THE DAUGHTERS OF
LUKE MCCALL

THE DAUGHTERS OF LUKE MCCALL

Linda Sandifer

Five Star
Unity, Maine

Five Star First Edition Romance Series.
Published in 2000 in conjunction with Multimedia Product Development, Inc.

Cover photograph by Robert Darby

Set in 11 pt. Plantin by Rick Gundberg.

Printed in the United States on permanent paper.

Library of Congress Cataloging-in-Publication Data

Sandifer, Linda.
    The daughters of Luke McCall / by Linda Sandifer.
        p.   cm. — (Five Star first edition romance series)
    ISBN 0-7862-2583-1 (hc : alk. paper)
    1. Fathers and daughters — Fiction. 2. Fugitives from justice — Fiction. 3. California — Fiction. 4. Outlaws — Fiction. I. Title. II. Series.
PS3569.A5165 D38   2000
    813′.54—dc21
                                                    00-035321

To Dona and Elaine
Sisters first, friends always

and

In Loving Memory
To Daddy

Contents

THE MEMOIRS OF DELANEY MCCALL
June 1, 1920 11

CHAPTER ONE
The Wild Bunch 14

CHAPTER TWO
Wrangling 24

CHAPTER THREE
A Back-Handed Trade 36

CHAPTER FOUR
Dodging the Loop 50

CHAPTER FIVE
Loose Cinch 57

CHAPTER SIX
Jumping Fences. 67

CHAPTER SEVEN
Crow-Hopping 82

CHAPTER EIGHT
Quittin' the Flat. 92

CHAPTER NINE
Clawing Leather. 100

CHAPTER TEN
Empty Saddle 112

CHAPTER ELEVEN
Leadin' Old Dan 123

CHAPTER TWELVE
High-Headed 133

CHAPTER THIRTEEN
Ground-Hitched 143

CHAPTER FOURTEEN
A Handful of Mane 150

CHAPTER FIFTEEN
A Foot in the Stirrup 157

CHAPTER SIXTEEN
In a Lather 171

CHAPTER SEVENTEEN
Cross-Hobbled 179

CHAPTER EIGHTEEN
Tightening the Cinch 191

CHAPTER NINETEEN
Choking Down 203

CHAPTER TWENTY
Takin' the Bit 210

CHAPTER TWENTY-ONE
Running Free 222

THE MEMOIRS OF DELANEY MCCALL
December 18, 1920 226

The Memoirs of Delaney McCall

JUNE 1, 1920

My sisters and I have been called everything from horse thieves to whores, and a number of invidious things in between. But once, a long time ago, there was a man who referred to us as the finest ladies he'd ever known. Now that was probably a wild stretch of his imagination, but if he wanted to believe that, it was all right by us. And I suppose we could act the part when we had a mind to—and the proper clothes.

I think the most common description of the four of us was "the daughters of Luke McCall." That said a lot in itself and people got a right smart image of us in just those five words. We were proud of the description and took to introducing ourselves that way. It opened a lot of doors. It closed a few too. But we were never once ashamed of it. No, we would have died to protect the name and the man. And we darn near did a time or two.

The only thing we really objected to was the way some Eastern-artist-come-West depicted us on those Wanted posters. Heck, me and Brett and Hank and Andy might have been a bit rough around the edges, like diamonds in the raw, but even with Colt .44's in hand we didn't look like men with long hair. No, both Mama and Daddy were too good-looking for us to turn out ugly. I guess we should have been thankful for that artist's unbecoming rendition of our faces. It saved our lives on more than one occasion.

There were those who wanted us dead, of course, and those who wanted to protect us. There were those who wanted us for financial

11

gain. And those who just wanted us. Yup, there were a few too many of those. But our allegiance was to each other, and to Daddy, and to a way of life that was slipping past us faster than the shadow of running mustangs across those golden California hills.

I tried hard to hold onto it, I can tell you that, but I was as helpless as a newborn calf in a Nevada snowstorm. Brett always told me I was just going to have to live with the change, but Hank didn't fault me for trying to hold on to the carefree days of our youth. No, Hank didn't fault me at all, because Hank understood me better than most.

Delaney lifted pen from paper and flexed her hand. The arthritis was acting up today. Probably a storm moving in off the ocean. It was always worse when the weather turned bad. Or maybe she just liked to believe that it ached less at times than at others. Maybe that was why she had sat down and started writing her memoirs in the first place. By forcing herself to think of who she once had been—young and vital and beautiful—it compensated a little for what she had become— old and frail and wrinkled. That and a need not to just let her life disappear from the face of the earth when her time was up. And it would be up soon. She could feel the time slipping away in some inner part of her that went much deeper than her bones.

It wasn't that her life had been anything out of the ordinary, at least in her opinion, except for that brief interlude when she and her sisters came upon that bend in the road, and, in following it, their lives had changed forever.

She wanted to go back—God, more than anything. She wanted to relive it. To get on Old Buck again and ride like the wind. She'd told the stories dozens of times, but the children and grandchildren never seemed to listen with more than half an ear. Funny how people only sought the future, never the past. They only sought the substance of their own lives and ignored all others.

Maybe it was for them that she wrote, so that someday one or two of them might open up the journal and read it and see things the way they'd been when she'd been a girl. There was some vanity involved too. She hated being just an old woman in their eyes, because she was so much more. Mainly, she wanted to go back, and remembering was the only way to do that. . . .

CHAPTER ONE

THE WILD BUNCH

Late September, 1863

The mustangs always came to the pool just before daybreak, in that serene hour before birds sing and breezes stir. Partially concealed by the half light, they would trot cautiously to the water's edge. They expected enemies at every turn, but still they would drink too much, filling their bellies until they were logy, because they knew it was a long time until sundown.

Delaney McCall watched the mustangs' dark flow of movement as the sun rose closer to the horizon. She tuned her ears to the low, distant rumble of their hooves across the dry autumn grass. Her nostrils detected the dust they stirred as it drifted up into the quiet air. In that dim hour, she knew her father and three sisters were in position in the Diablo hills, even though she could not see them.

Hidden in a little grove of trees, she settled deeper into her high-backed California saddle and tugged her hat down tighter on her forehead. There was only one easy way out of Wild Horse Canyon, but those mustangs weren't going to find it today.

The horses milled around the watering hole for thirty minutes, then they started getting restless just as the sky took color. When the young stallion, a yellow dun, lifted his nose to the east, Delaney knew he'd picked up their scent.

She tightened her reins, preparing for the run. Her buckskin felt the shift of her body, and his muscles bunched in anticipation of flight. But Buck was trained not to move until Delaney gave the signal, so he remained stock-still.

"He's gonna run, Daddy," she whispered anxiously. "What in tarnation are you waitin' for?"

As if he had heard her thoughts from across the distance, Luke McCall appeared atop the eastern hills, a dark silhouette against a pink and orange sky. Then he was moving, leaning out fully along the neck of his gray, Old Dan, as it raced hell-bent down the long, golden hills. To the left and the right, and the left again, came three more riders. Hank on her black gelding, Brett and Andy on their sorrels. They came as quietly as riders could at full gallop.

The stallion saw them and his shrill bugle of warning split the serenity of the valley. The lead mare wheeled and drove the other mares away from the water. But the easy way from the canyon was blocked by the riders. They were forced to turn west again, toward the trees where Delaney was hidden.

Closer they thundered. It was crucial that they did not see her until they were in the trees, running for the rocky incline that switch-backed out of the canyon. Just over the crest of the hills was a long valley that ran for a mile toward a rocky rise. Over that rise, the land narrowed down into another valley, a narrower one that was hemmed in by a thick patch of oaks. The McCalls had opened up a path through the trees that would funnel the horses directly into a blind corral that they had painstakingly built at the end.

The buckskin was raring to go by the time the mares and stallion flowed up over the hills in tight formation. Luke and Delaney's three sisters raced in behind the mustangs, keeping them moving toward what they believed was their only escape.

Delaney's timing had to be perfect. Too soon and she

risked turning them back. Too late and they could circle around and get past the other riders. She waited until they had topped the rise. Then she leaned forward in the saddle and gave the buckskin his head. He shot into a gallop, knowing exactly what to do.

With riders seemingly coming at them from all directions, the mustangs dove for the path in the trees. Luke and her sisters surged up over the ridge. They headed down the grassy side just a few lengths behind Delaney, gaining the momentum that would be needed to stay with the mustangs and keep them from veering away from the trap at the last minute.

Andy and Brett, the twins, raced alongside the mustangs on the left. Hank joined Delaney on the right. Luke McCall drove them hard and fast from the rear, never allowing them the space to circle back to freedom. Delaney and her buckskin raced close enough to the mustangs to feel the heat of their tiring bodies as she and the others forced them into the stand of oaks. With their every outlet cut off now, the broomtails necked down into the man-made path.

"We've got 'em now!" Luke called out victoriously.

The horses thundered into the blind corral. The confused young stallion skidded to a stop, followed by his band of mares and colts. Seeing he had been tricked, he whirled and ran frantically along the enclosure, shrieking his anger and defiance. He tore back in the direction he had come, looking for escape, but Delaney and Hank and Luke blocked the narrow escape while Andy and Brett leaped from their saddles and threw poles across the narrow opening.

Luke sat back in his saddle. With his blood still pumping, and the excitement of the chase still wild in his eyes, he took off his hat and wiped the sweat from his brow. "Well, there's another pay day, girls. After breakfast I'll head over to Breckenridge's and tell him his men can come and get them

16

any time. Then I'll ride into town and see if Stark has our money yet."

"Don't let Stark put you off any longer, Daddy." Brett's jaw set firmly. "He's just about worn out that friendship he boasts so much about."

"Six months is long enough," Andy agreed. "He's the only one we've ever let take horses without money up front, and then he tries to weasel out of paying us altogether."

"If he doesn't have the money this time, he'll have to give the horses back," Luke assured them. "I've already decided that."

"You're too nice to him." Delaney crossed her forearms over her saddle horn. "I would have shown him which way was up a long time ago."

"Like I've said before, girls, me and Eli go back a long way. He saved your mother's life. None of you would have been born if he hadn't. So it's kinda hard to get rough with him."

"He has our gratitude for what he did for Mama, but he can't use that to take advantage of us for the rest of our lives."

"You're right, Delaney, but there's something else, too," Luke reminded them. "Eli Stark is a cruel man by nature. Couple that with being the marshal of Hawk's Point, and it's not a good idea to rankle him. Don't get me wrong. I'm not afraid of him. I could whip the stuffings out of him. But he's like a dog that might bite you one day and lick your face the next."

Delaney pushed her hat to the back of her head. "I think he's got an upstairs hinge that was never tightened down."

"He's using that badge to keep from paying up," Hank said tightly. "He figures nobody can touch him as long as he's wearing it. We're not the only ones he owes money to. I hear he's charged so much over at Pearson's General Store that old man Pearson is considering shutting him off. But Pearson is afraid of him, like everybody else around Hawk's Point. Why, he's even got Mrs. Jacobs afraid to kick him out of her boarding house. From what I gather, he hasn't paid her in months. He's running roughshod over that town like he owns it and everybody in it."

Andy drew her foot up out of the stirrup and curled her knee around the saddle horn. "He's *trying* to own it by buying up half the businesses. Then he claims he's 'short of cash' when it comes time to pay his bills."

"Well, let's worry about Stark later," Delaney grumbled. "Right now, I'd welcome the sight of a dozen eggs and a side of bacon. I feel like a Digger Indian. Half-starved."

As they left the blind corral for camp, daylight broke above the Diablos. Like the shadow beneath the outstretched wings of an eagle, its golden glow raced westward, warming the backs of the five victorious riders.

Luke McCall rode into Hawk's Point, his thoughts crowded with memories of Melinda. The past intruded a lot these days when he wasn't engaged in something that took all his concentration. It was hard to believe that she'd been dead nineteen years now. Sometimes he had the feeling he could just go back to their six-room adobe in Monterey and find her there, waiting to curl up by his side and listen to all his grand adventures. At least he'd had seven years with her, and he owed those years to Eli Stark.

Luke pulled rein in front of the lawman's office and swung to the ground. He looped the reins over the hitching rail and stepped onto the boardwalk. Through the open door of the marshal's office, Stark heard boot heels scrape on the boardwalk. He automatically reached for the six-shooter resting on his desk, but relaxed when he saw it was Luke.

"Why so jumpy, Eli?" Luke stepped inside.

Stark shrugged shoulders that had grown massive with age. "Seems there's always some low-life hankering to take down a lawman." He looked past Luke, expectantly. "Didn't you bring those pretty daughters?"

"They're out keeping an eye on a new bunch of mustangs we just caught this morning." Luke tried being cordial. He really hoped he wouldn't have to get snotty with Stark.

The marshal returned the revolver to the desktop then ambled over to the coffee pot perched atop the pot-bellied stove. He filled two cups and handed one to Luke. "I suppose you and those daughters have nearly cleaned out the mustangs around here."

Luke chuckled, cradling the hot cup in his callused hands. "We haven't even come close."

Stark returned to his chair and ran a hand through gray-streaked hair that had once been sandy brown. He was a big man and he liked to use his size to intimidate people. It was a trait Luke had never liked in him. Among others.

The marshal had courted Melinda first. Then he'd taken a bullet for her during that shootout in Los Angeles that had killed three innocent bystanders.

Melinda had ended the courtship with Eli about the time Luke came to town. It had been a sore spot Stark had picked at until it had become a festering wound. He was still picking, nearly twenty-six years later.

"I suppose you're here for your money," Stark commented jovially enough. "You never come by these days unless it's business."

Luke sipped at the coffee. "It's been six months, Eli."

"You know I'm good for the money. I paid you for that other bunch of mustangs last year."

"I know, but I don't extend credit to anybody else, and I

can't let it go on any longer, even for you. I've got a living to make."

Eli remained pleasantly accommodating. "And I certainly do appreciate your patience with me, Luke. A marshal doesn't make much money, and, as you probably know, I've been expanding in some of my enterprises, trying to have something to support myself when I quit this job in a few years. I didn't forget about you. I had the money right there in my safe, planning on paying it to you the next time you came into town. Then I got a letter from my sister down in Texas and she needed money real bad. The men have gone off to fight those Yankees and the women are having to fend for themselves. I sent every dime I had just last week. Hell, I'm worried it'll get stolen and she'll never see it. Before it's over, I might have to go down there and help her and the kids until this war is over."

Luke didn't know if Eli even had a sister. If he didn't, it was a good lie, one intended to play on a man's conscience and sympathy.

"Just give me another month or two and I should have some more," Stark continued confidently, as if he hadn't heard a word Luke had said.

Luke rose and sauntered to the open door, leaning a shoulder against the frame while watching the movements of the townspeople on main street. He sipped at his coffee. "I'm going to have to take the horses back, Eli," he said as casually as if he'd commented on the weather. "I can't extend credit to you any longer."

It was a moment before the silence behind him was broken. "Well, hell, Luke, if you're that hard up for money, I'll go take out a loan at the bank."

Luke's patience was borderline. He cast the marshal a baleful look from over his shoulder and set his cup on the window sill. "I'm not hard up for money, but I'm not in the business to give mustangs away, not even to the local law. If you don't have the money by now then you leave me no choice but to take the horses back."

"You didn't say you were going to do that."

"That's what usually happens when you have something you can't pay for, Eli. My daughters and I will come and get them tomorrow. Do you still have them out on your place?"

Eli leaned his chair back on two legs as if nothing had changed between them. "They're still there, but I've had them branded and green broke, put quite a bit of money into them. You'll have to reimburse me for that."

Instantly Eli saw the sparks leap into Luke's eyes, and he knew he'd pushed the mustanger a step too far. He lifted a hand to the air as if to brush the whole thing off. "Oh, never mind about that, Luke. I'll just take the loss. Do what you have to do."

"I intend to."

Luke was to the hitching rail when Eli called him back. The marshal took the position against the door jamb that Luke had vacated. Rolling a toothpick around in his teeth, he said, "One more thing, Luke. You still haven't told me whether Henrietta has agreed to let me come courtin'. God, if she don't remind me of Melinda."

Luke's gut knotted along with his fists. "I told you before, Eli, you're too old to be courtin' my daughter."

"Why not let her be the one to decide whether I'm too old or not. After all, she's crowding twenty-five, ain't she? Now, don't go get mad at me, Luke, but what with you raisin' those girls like boys, you might have just sealed their fate as far as them ever gettin' husbands. Ain't many men who want a gal that strides around in pants and rides astraddle."

"They can ride sidesaddle when the occasion calls for it.

They can even do it while balancing a parasol in one hand. If I've taught them anything, it's to take care of themselves. I don't figure that's anything to be ashamed of."

"Oh, I didn't say it was. It's just that most people wouldn't agree with you. Listen, Luke. I'll give you double for those horses if you let me court Henrietta. Triple, if she marries me."

Luke unwound the reins from the hitching rail and stepped into the saddle. "Hank isn't interested in courting you, and I'm not interested in promised money."

"The way I see it, you owe me."

"How do you figure?"

"Because of Melinda. Sometimes I think you befriended me just so's you could meet her."

"Melinda wouldn't have married you even if I hadn't come along."

Stark's eyes narrowed. "Did she tell you that?"

"She did."

Stark didn't like the truth and chose to ignore it. "Well, that's water under the bridge, and Henrietta isn't getting any younger. She's already a spinster by most standards. You ought to be happy I want to take her off your hands. I guess maybe I'll just have to ask her myself."

Luke forced his horse up onto the boardwalk and forced Stark back into the safety of the door frame. "If you get within ten feet of Hank, or any of my girls, I'll string you up. I've seen the way you treat women, Eli, and it is not commendable."

"Is that any way to talk to a friend?"

"You and I took a few drinks together on Saturday night when we were young men. We played some card games and raised a little cane. Don't make more of it than it was."

Eli stood in the doorway and watched him ride away. Luke

felt the marshal's eyes boring into his back until he was out of the man's sight. He hadn't wanted to make an enemy of Eli Stark, but he'd sure enough had his fill of doin' the two-step with him.

CHAPTER TWO

WRANGLING

Luke McCall seldom stayed in town after dark. He'd always told his daughters that there was nothing to be gained by it except the acquisition of a mess of trouble. But the sun hovered on the blazing lip of the western horizon, preparing to vanish from view, and still he had not returned.

Delaney paced through the scrub brush near the camp fire. She paused occasionally to listen for the syncopated rhythm of Old Dan approaching on a lope down the long hills. She flared her nostrils, like a young colt trying to detect the scent of danger. All she smelled was the musky odor of the mustangs' sweat and manure, and the dust from their milling hooves as they crowded together in the blind corral, frenzied from their loss of freedom. All she heard were their frightened squeals above the lyrical and nonsensical chatter of her three sisters gathered around the camp fire.

Hank tended the fire and the stew. Andy played a losing game of solitaire. Brett was fixed on her perfect reflection in a gilt-framed hand mirror that had once belonged to their mother, trying to decide if she liked what she saw. If the lighting was just right, she might be pacified.

It was mostly the loquacious Brett whose voice rose above the din in the corral as she dreamed aloud of a fancy dress she'd seen two weeks ago in a San Francisco store window. Their daddy, who was the only person aside from Hank who had recollection of the twins' childhood, claimed that Brett had been born talking. All Delaney knew was that the oldest of the twins definitely seemed to hold an aversion to silence. As a matter of fact, Brett had carried the nickname Gabby until, at the age of twelve, she'd rebelled and told them all in no uncertain terms that if any of them called her that again she would shoot them. She'd had their daddy's old Baby Dragoon revolver in her hand at the time, so no one used the sobriquet again.

They'd all seen the dress in Lady Millicent's Dress Shop and fallen in love with it, but Brett was prone to laying claims to things and putting them off-limits to anybody else, even if she couldn't have them herself. The rest of them hadn't put up a fuss about it. A dress in a window wasn't worth bickering over and it certainly wasn't something Delaney herself would have a hankering to wear. No, that dress would have required a corset tighter than the birth canal of a one-year old Longhorn heifer.

"Don't you think Daddy would have a hissy fit if he saw you in that plunging neckline?" Andy laid a queen of hearts on a king of spades and didn't look up. Her eyes roamed the cards instead, searching for her next move.

Nobody knew exactly why, but Andy could usually turn a winning hand at just about any card game she sat down to play. She was especially proficient at Poker, Black Jack, and Red Dog. Solitaire was a little tougher, but she still won often enough that she didn't disgrace herself. When she wasn't playing cards, she was reading. She seldom sat idle. Like Hank, she didn't seem to be inflicted with the pent-up energy that kept Brett and Delaney constantly moving.

"I'm twenty-two and he can't tell me what to wear anymore," Brett replied matter-of-factly. Her eyes never left her reflection in the mirror. "With what I've saved, and with my share of the money from this herd of mustangs, I'm going to hire Lady Millicent to duplicate that dress for me."

Unwavering in her determination, Brett dampened the tip of her forefinger with her tongue and pushed up a dark brown eyebrow, so in contrast to her blond hair, in the hopes of training it to grow upward in an arch. She'd been going through these same motions for years, to no avail. Delaney would never vocalize it, but she had decided that Brett's eyebrows were the only thing on her face that weren't perfect. Because of it, Brett wouldn't go to the outhouse without her tweezers. Well, maybe that was an exaggeration, but she certainly guarded the instrument as if it were made of gold.

Delaney was thinking about the dress again. In her estimation, it would be a waste of money to buy something that would end up hanging in the cherrywood armoire back in their small adobe in Monterey—the place they called home but had seldom seen these last few years. And it truly perplexed her as to why a woman would want to be seen in public with half of her bosom exposed anyway, even if it was the style.

"What do you want with a danged silk dress, Brett?" Delaney suddenly spouted, having lost patience with the entire matter. "Your toes are nearly sticking out of your boots and you'll be having to put patches on your best pair of britches here pretty soon. *Wanting* just for the sake of wanting is non-productive, a waste of good money."

Brett pursed her lips then opened them again with a click of her tongue. "Just because you have no aspirations aside from chasing wild horses, Delaney, does not mean that the rest of us are so dull. Mustanging is hard and dirty. Frankly, I'd rather be under a parasol strolling down a street in Paris, turning the head of every male that passes."

Delaney's face screwed up. "To what end? Just to know you can do it?"

"No, you idiot. To find a rich man to marry. Daddy isn't going to be around forever to take care of us."

"But why would a rich man want a poor girl?"

"Because he simply could not resist the temptation of my outstanding beauty and charm. And for love, too, of course."

Delaney contemplated that idea for a long moment. "But why would a rich man want a woman for love if she had only married *him* for his money?"

Brett's temper flared. "Can't you enjoy the fantasy of romance?"

Delaney shook her head. "It truly escapes me, Brett."

"Well, I'll tell you something, Delaney. I ride like a man chasing these broomtails because I have no choice at this point in my life. It doesn't mean I intend to spend the rest of my life with my derriere bumping leather."

"You can't spend your whole life fluttering your eyelashes at men either. One day you might just catch one and then you'll have to settle down to babies and household drudgeries that will make mustanging look like a buggy ride in the country."

"Not if I marry a rich man and have plenty of servants."

"You could just make your own money," Andy put in logically. "Daddy always said that it's not wise to hang your star on a man. I guess he knows what he's talking about, him being a man."

"That confirms my suspicions," Delaney said dryly.

Brett glanced up long enough to give her an annoyed perusal. "What confirms your suspicions?"

"That in the case of twins, only one gets the brains. In this case, it wasn't you."

Andy grinned. "I've always thought the same thing myself, Delaney."

Brett wouldn't let anything die until she had gotten in the

last word. "You're nineteen now, Delaney—a *woman,* just in case you hadn't noticed. Why don't you try acting like one?"

"Well, ma'am, if being a woman means parading up and down the street holding up both ends of a silk dress, then I'd rather just stay right here in the hills until I die."

"And you probably will. As an old maid."

Delaney's temper reached its limits. "How can you even care about such things right now?" she challenged, her eyes narrowing angrily at all three of them for not being the least bit concerned about their father's tardiness. "It's almost dark and Daddy's not back. He could be lying dead in town right now with a bullet through his heart and here you're talking about blue silk dresses!"

"Why should we all sit around with knotted brows, worrying ourselves sick when you do enough worrying for twenty people?" Brett countered. "You always imagine the worst, Delaney. Daddy is probably just enjoying a drink and maybe some female companionship. Did you ever think of that? He's a man, you know. One, I might add, who is still handsome."

It was useless to argue with Brittany McCall; the woman was tenacious. Delaney would never be able to make her understand anything of what she felt inside, of what drove her, anymore than she would be able to fully comprehend the mechanisms of Brett's brain. In her heart, Delaney clung to her father. Her greatest fear was losing him. Without him she would be alone in a way that even the companionship of her sisters could not alleviate. She had never known her mother. It was said that you don't miss what you've never had, but Delaney did miss being held in the arms of the woman who had given her life. She was to blame for her mother's death, and there was no getting around it. If she had never been born, then their mother would still be alive.

"I'm thinking maybe I should head toward town and meet

him. Make sure he's all right."

"Daddy is a grown man," Brett said, tucking the precious mirror back into her saddlebags. Even though the mirror belonged to them all, Brett insisted on keeping it in her possession. She didn't believe the others could keep from breaking it. "He can take care of himself. When are you going to quit being such a mother hen where he's concerned?"

Andy laid the cards out on her blanket for another game. Hank seldom interfered with Delaney and Brett's little tiffs, unless they got completely out of hand, but Andy always felt compelled to play peacemaker. "Brett's right, Delaney. Daddy could very well have a lady friend at Hawk's Point or San Jose. I've noticed that when he rides into town, any town, no woman can deny herself a long, wistful look. I'd like to meet a man as handsome as Daddy someday. I wouldn't care if he wasn't rich either, just as long as he loved me and treated me like I was the most important thing in his life."

Where Brett locked horns with Delaney and tried to force her around to her way of thinking, Andy tried subtle persuasion with a smile. They were all dreamers in their way, but Andy was the true romantic whose thoughts and concerns were always gentle ones. You couldn't be mean to Andy. There was that kindness in her eyes that prevented it. And Andy couldn't be mean back. Delaney couldn't even remember more than a few times that Andy had even been upset enough to raise her voice.

"If a grown man could honestly take care of himself, ladies, then God wouldn't have had to create Woman," Delaney replied smartly. "It says right in the Bible that Adam needed a helpmate."

"He created Woman for procreation, you ninny." Brett again.

"Yes, but he said specifically that Adam needed someone to look out for him."

The wind shifted and Brett got a face full of smoke and ashes. Swearing and waving it away, she stood up and headed toward the thick trees where they had built the blind corral. "This conversation has turned stale as the heel on week-old bread. I'm going to check the horses and see if that stallion will come up to me."

Hank's brows suddenly shot together as she entered the conversation. "Be careful around him, Brett. His first thought is a way out of that corral, and he won't be happy to see one of the people who put him there."

"Oh, he's just scared and mad as the devil. Don't worry, I'll stay on the opposite side of the fence."

"I'll go with you," Andy said, abandoning her cards and hurrying to catch up with her twin. She had always felt the need to protect Brett from her own recklessness.

Delaney watched the two of them stride away. For somebody who wanted to be a lady, Brett could walk like a longshoreman when she took a notion to cover a lot of ground. As for Andy, she was just so used to being a part of Brett that she didn't know what to do with herself when Brett wasn't by her side.

The two of them looked like peas in a pod. Both were tall and blond, green-eyed and shapely. Even in men's clothes, and covered from top to bottom with trail dust, they had a way of dressing and had a certain carriage, that turned every man's head who came within eyesight of them.

As for Hank and Delaney. Well, Hank looked like their mother in the face, and even had her golden brown hair and hazel eyes. Her coloring was softer, less dramatic than that of the twins', like morning sunshine touching on a field of autumn grass.

Delaney was the black sheep of the bunch. She'd ended up with Daddy's black hair and blue eyes, even his features. She had never had anybody tell her she was pretty, the way they had Hank and the twins, but some old biddy in town one day had called her "handsome." Delaney figured it would have been a better compliment if she hadn't been a girl.

"The battle might be lost, my willful baby sister, but not the war."

Delaney turned back to the camp fire and met Hank's indulgent smile. "I didn't lose."

"Didn't you?" Hank's eyebrows arched above amused, omniscient eyes. "I don't think anybody has ever had a full and satisfying victory over Brett. Come here. Help me roll this dough into biscuits and get them into the Dutch oven. Daddy should be coming along any time now. He doesn't like to ride after dark unless the moon is full, and it won't be tonight."

"My point exactly." Delaney released a sigh, and with it all the pent-up anger. She sauntered over to Hank and joined her on the fallen log where she'd set up her "kitchen." Hank had pretty much raised Delaney. After Delaney got older and was smart enough to give life some consideration, she had wondered if Hank had ever resented being forced into motherhood at a tender age, but Delaney had never found any tell-tale signs that she had. Hank had always loved her unconditionally.

Hank lifted the lid on her stew to stir and sample it. It was only a concoction of potatoes, venison, and onions, but Hank had a knack wih seasonings and she never went on the trail without bringing along pouches of such herbs as garlic, thyme, chives, or sage. She'd sprinkle a little of this, a little of that, and the food always came out tasting better than anything you could buy at the most elite restaurants in San Francisco or Sacramento.

They'd been to both cities numerous times on horse trading trips, and Daddy always took them to an expensive restaurant that required their best clothes. "A person needs to be versed in all aspects of life," he would say. "You girls especially need to know how to conduct yourselves. Your mother wouldn't be happy with me if I was lax in your up-bringing. She was a fine lady and she would want her daugh-ters to be the same. It's commendable for a woman to be able to run down wild mustangs—don't misunderstand me, and I know for a fact that sons couldn't have been better riders—but it is essential that a woman know how to dress properly, fix up her hair, and conduct herself in a ladylike fashion when she's in public."

"Quit worrying about him." Hank's soft, smiling repri-mand drew Delaney to her haunches next to her. "He'll be okay."

Delaney accepted Hank calling her down, for she always did it in a polite manner, but it rankled when Brett or any-body else did it, except Daddy, that is.

"Sometimes a man needs time away from his children, Delaney," Hank continued. "He's probably having a drink or two, just like Brett said. Maybe even spending some time at Lizzie's. He'll be along directly."

Delaney washed her hands in the basin next to the fire. "Do you really think Daddy visits the whores? I mean, I just can't see him doing that."

Hank smiled in her quiet, tolerant way. "And why can't you visualize him being amorous with a woman? He's still a handsome man."

Delaney set her jaw but made one concession. "I guess that's fine just as long as he doesn't marry one and bring her home. I won't have some strange woman trying to change things and boss us all around."

"He's got a right to happiness, Delaney, and we're all getting to the age where we should be getting married and out on our own anyway. We're all old maids as it is."

"I'm only nineteen, and I can tell you I'm not ready to be tied down to a man and a bunch of squawling babies. I'd have to give up mustanging, and I'll be hanged before I do that. We all need to stick together. Family is the only thing that any of us has in the end. Besides, who would Daddy get to help him catch mustangs if we all went off and got married?"

Hank studied Delaney with a look that was much too serious. "Sooner or later we're all going to go our separate way, Delaney. You might as well accept that. It's a part of life."

"I'm not going to get married. I won't have a man telling me what I can and cannot do, or choosing the life I live." Delaney's forehead furrowed like the rows in old Juan Castillo's corn patch down on the Salinas. Having made her indisputable declaration, she dried her hands on the hand towel, took up some dough, and started molding baking powder biscuits. With practiced expertise, she placed them in the bottom of a Dutch oven.

"As for Daddy visiting Lizzie's," she spoke in her usual adamant tone, "he wouldn't dishonor Mama that way. I know he wouldn't. He loves her more than anything. Did you know that he still takes out that old locket with Mama's picture and just sits and stares at it?"

Hank shook her head, not in response to Delaney's question, but in response to a knowledge she possessed about her younger sister. She had, after all, raised her. She knew her better than anyone. Knew what drove her, what hurt her, what made her happy, what didn't. She worried about Delaney because the girl had taken to the wild like a mustang, and there was the possibility that she would be even harder to tame. A young colt could be taught compliance, to even forget his freedom, but Delaney McCall would be like that stallion. She would go down fighting.

"It doesn't matter that Daddy still loves our mother and always will. The living have to go on living."

"We shouldn't be talking about Daddy this way." Delaney worked furiously shaping the dough into balls and then pressing them flat between the palms of her hands. "It's disrespectful. If we keep it up we'll be too embarrassed to even look him in the eye when he gets back."

Hank's gaze searched the darkening hills. "He'll be along soon." Her words were confident, but concern knotted the center of her brow.

It's all Delaney needed. She jumped up. "I'm going looking for him."

Hank caught her arm. "No. Daddy left us here to watch these horses and make sure they don't break out of the corral and to make sure renegades don't come swooping in here and steal them. You know it isn't the most invincible structure we've ever built, and that stallion doesn't like being caught one little bit. Why don't you play us a tune on your harmonica, something soft and soothing. This stew and the biscuits should be ready in thirty minutes or so. Besides, Delaney, it's probably not wise for you to head into town alone."

"I can handle myself. Any man tries to take advantage of me and I'll put a bullet in him."

The twins were returning and caught the tail-end of the conversation. Brett piped up, "You would never have to worry about that happening, little sister. No man would ever guess there was a female body lurking under that get-up you're wearing."

Delaney's chin jutted defensively. "At least I'm not weighed down with so much fringe and frippery that I look like a walking dry goods store! Why, your horse can't even run fast enough to scatter his own shit for having to pack all your paraphernalia."

Andy rolled her eyes. "Here we go again."

Hank suddenly stood up, thrusting out a hand in a gesture that demanded silence. "Hush! All of you," she commanded in a rough whisper. "Somebody's coming. Maybe Daddy."

But they all knew it could just as easily be somebody else. In silent unison, they melted into the shadows, their .44s scraping leather.

CHAPTER THREE

A BACK-HANDED TRADE

The rider came in on a fast walk, cast in silhouette before he reached the light of the fire. Delaney breathed a sigh of relief because it was their Daddy, sure enough. She holstered her revolver and stepped from her hiding place along with her sisters.

Luke McCall halted his big gray a few feet from the fire and dismounted. He looked as mad as a skinned rattlesnake that's just crawled up on a hot rock, and Delaney knew right away that things hadn't gone well with Marshal Stark.

He hunkered down next to the fire and poured himself a cup of coffee. "We're getting those horses back tomorrow," he said with no preliminaries. "Eli wouldn't pay up. Had some lame excuse about sending all his money to his sister in Texas."

He sipped at the coffee while Hank dished him up a plate of stew. "I would have thought he'd cough up the money, given an ultimatum."

"He paid to have them green-broke. Wanted me to reimburse him for that."

Andy settled next to him on the fallen log. "I'd say he has his priorities mixed up."

Luke's brow wrinkled with something akin to worry and regret. "I'm afraid I made an enemy of him today, girls. It wasn't a smart thing to do, knowing his mean streak."

"It's about time somebody stood up to him," Hank assured him. "Don't worry, Dad. He can't do anything to us for taking back what's rightfully ours."

"Never underestimate Eli Stark. He can cause us grief if he's a mind to."

"I'll feed that side-wheeler a fatal pill if he comes near me," Delaney proclaimed. "I have no qualms about it."

"Killing a man is easier said than done, Delaney," he replied dismally.

He ate his supper in contemplative quiet. When he was finished, he set his plate aside and looked hard at Hank. "I wasn't going to say anything to you, Hank, because I didn't want to trouble you. But I guess it's time you knew that Stark's got the eye for you. Apparently you remind him of your mother, and he never got over losing her. So don't be misled by any sweet talk he might feed you. He can be charming if he wants something, but he's mean and dishonest to the core. Always has been. He wouldn't treat a wife any better than he treats his horses, which isn't saying much."

Hank shifted uneasily. "I guess that explains why he has always looked at me the way he has. Makes me chill all over."

Silence fell over the McCalls; each slipped into private musings over what had transpired. Luke hadn't wanted to frighten them, but he had always tried to prepare them for whatever life might throw at them.

He stood up. "I'll take one last look at the mustangs. You girls get some sleep. We've got a big day ahead of us tomorrow. It'll come soon enough."

At daybreak, Delaney leaned over from her saddle and threw open the gate at Eli Stark's corral. The mustangs saw the opening and fled their confinement with tails high and hooves flying. They hadn't been so long from freedom that they'd forgotten it.

Eli Stark came out of his week-end cabin long enough to acknowledge their presence. He said, "It gets around about a man who reneges on his deals, McCall. You'll regret this sooner or later." Then he went back inside and closed the door.

Delaney took the lead, hazing the horses on a lope across the hills to Bart Breckinridge's ranch. Luke and Hank took drag. The twins took the flank positions. Five miles from Eli Stark's corral they slowed to a trot and held it.

Luke hadn't discussed it with Breckenridge, but he had a hunch that the young rancher would buy these horses as well as the ones they'd captured yesterday. These would be particularly appealing for him to add to his remuda since they were already green-broke. He figured he could get them to Bart's by noon, then get the others over there before nightfall.

By mid-morning, the horses were tiring and alternating their paces between a walk and a trot. Any hope of shedding their captors had been lost. Only one of the bangtails tried consistently to break from the herd and his captors. His contentious behavior was enough to thin Delaney's patience. She finally announced that she would pay Breckinridge herself for that one if her daddy would let her put a bullet between his sorry eyes.

Luke McCall just grinned and said, "Patience, Delaney. You know there is always one rotten spud in the bottom of every gunny sack."

"Yes, and you also told us to dig down until we find it and toss it out before the rest of them taters get spoiled too."

"We only have a few miles to go," Luke humored her. "We'll let Breckenridge deal with that churn-head. He doesn't believe there's such a thing as a bad horse."

"He's still young."

Hank left her position on drag and joined Luke and Delaney. Half-turned in the saddle, her eyes were pinned on something behind them. "Riders coming up fast, Dad," she announced. "At least a dozen."

Sensing trouble, Delaney's heart started pumping like a piston. "That many riders usually spells trouble."

Andy and Brett loped up next to them. "That roan out in the lead looks like the one Stark rides," Andy said.

"What would he be doing here with a dozen riders?" Brett voiced the thought running through five minds. Her brow was creased with concern. "Somebody must have robbed the bank or something."

"Bunch the horses in that coulee until we find out what's going on." Luke McCall sat calmly with a poker face, but Delaney knew his muscles were taut and ready beneath the cool facade.

The McCalls were five abreast with rifles drawn by the time the group of twelve thundered to a stop in front of them and fanned out in a semi-circle. It was Stark all right, and he had that snake-eye face he wore more times than not. His badge seemed unusually bright in the morning light as he drew rein. Every rider with him was also sporting a star and a drawn revolver.

"What's going on here, Eli?" Luke asked, hoping civility would keep things calm. But one look at Stark's smug face and Luke knew better. A double-knot tightened in the pit of his stomach.

Stark sat business-like in his high-back saddle with his hands folded over the horn. A drawn Remington six-shot rested in his palm, pointed idly at Luke. "You know, Luke, you and I go back a fair piece. I never would have thought you'd do such an underhanded thing to an old friend. But here we sit, living proof."

"If we're going to talk, Eli, you're going to have to make some sense."

"Come on, Luke. Don't play games with me. You've been caught red-handed with stolen property. *Mine*. If you'll look close, you'll see my brand on those ponies you've bunched over in that gully. Now me and the boys here are going to have to bring you and your daughters in for stealing those horses, unless you have a bill of sale for them from me. Which I'm sure you don't because I didn't sell them to you."

"Why, you low-life sonofa—" Delaney rose out of the saddle as if she was going to kill him with her bare hands. "We didn't steal those horses!"

"It's all right, Delaney." Luke reached out, signaling her to stay calm and quiet. "We'll get to the bottom of this."

Delaney swallowed the rest of the words boiling up inside her throat. She was seeing red, but she realized that one act of aggression might be all Stark needed to have his posse open fire on them. Her dad knew it, too, and was offering her a graceful excuse to be quiet.

Luke had a temper like Delaney's, but time and experience had enabled him to put it on a longer fuse. "I suspect that what you've told these men is a dilly of a fabrication, Eli. You and I both know you couldn't pay me what you owed me for these horses and you agreed to let me take them back. You stood right there this morning on your front porch and watched me and my daughters drive them off."

Eli chuckled. "I didn't know you had such storytelling abilities, old friend, but you won't talk yourself out of this one. I have a bill of sale right here"—he pulled a piece of folded paper from his shirt pocket—"that says I paid you in full for fifteen head of mustangs. And you've signed it. Here, take a look for yourself and see if it jars your memory."

He hadn't given Stark a bill of sale for this bunch of mustangs, although he had for the others he'd sold him the year before. He was curious to see what Stark had come up with— a forgery, maybe?—so he took the proffered paper. But, sure enough, it was his handwriting on the seller's line. A closer examination revealed that the date, written with a pencil, had been rubbed out and changed to coincide with the day six months ago when Eli had taken possession of the horses in question.

"You've rubbed out the date on this, Eli, and then changed it. This is the bill of sale from our previous transaction."

"You'd better be careful who you're calling a liar and a cheat, Luke. I'm the law, remember? Also remember that you changed that date yourself. You wrote it wrong and had to fix it. Maybe you should have written it in ink and there wouldn't be any question about it now."

"A pencil was all either one of us had, Eli, and I *didn't* change the date."

"Can your daughters vouch for that?"

"You know as well as I do that they weren't with me on either of the sales."

"It appears to be your word against mine then. We're going to have to take you in, and those daughters of yours too."

Luke's eyes turned deadly. "You leave my girls out of this."

Stark shrugged. "They're all adults and clearly implicated in this crime. You'll all have your day in court, but I suspect you'll all hang, side by side.

"Now, throw down those guns—and any others you've got hidden on your persons. We don't want to be obliged to have

41

to shoot any of you. It's a pity you've led your beautiful daughters astray, Luke. They could have had promising futures as wives and mothers."

"We haven't done anything wrong, Dad," Hank objected, coming to full attention in the saddle. "He can't do this!"

Luke's angry gaze sliced into Stark. "This isn't about these horses at all. Is it, Eli?"

Stark just smiled smugly and glanced from Hank back to Luke. "Like I said, Luke, you'll have your day in court."

The five McCalls filled every cell in Eli Stark's jail. Hank and Delaney in one, the twins in another, and Luke a third.

"You might think you're pulling a fast one, Stark," Luke said as Stark turned the key in the lock, "but before this is over, I can promise you, you'll pay."

"What can you do dangling from the end of a rope, old pal? What are any of you going to do?"

He settled himself on his chair and propped his feet up on his desk. They could see him through the open door separating his office from the cells. He took out his pocket knife and started cleaning the dirt out from under his fingernails. "There *is* a way you can get out of here, Luke. I suppose you'd like to hear it."

"I'm not interested in what a double-crosser has to say. The trial will prove my innocence."

"Not necessarily. For a case like this, I think you can be assured that the jury is going to come from this town, and, in case you hadn't noticed, I pretty much own this town. The judge and I take supper together when he comes to sit the bench. But, like I was saying, I could drop these charges right now if you would reconsider what we were talking about earlier."

"I'll hang before I'll turn my daughter over to you, Stark."

"Maybe you would, but maybe they don't want to hang because of your foolish pride. And they *will* hang, McCall. I can assure you of that. Boy, wouldn't that draw people from all over? The hanging of four notorious female horse thieves could bring in a lot of money to Hawk's Point. Almost as good as a circus."

He dropped his feet to the floor with a thud and stood up, pocketing the knife. He sauntered over to the cell Hank and Delaney were sharing. "Ain't that right, girls? I'll bet you'd do just about anything to get out of this place. Why, you look like you got trapped in your own blind corral. Like wild young mustangs, scared to death, at the mercy of their captors."

Delaney had been pacing; she stopped and went up to the bars, curling her fingers around them in a death grip. "We McCalls stick together, marshal. We won't strike any deals with you."

"Well, now. I've heard two opinions, I think I'd like to hear what these two pretty blond-haired look-alikes have to say."

Andy had stretched full-length on one of the cots and didn't bother to lift her head from the pillow. It wasn't clean, and she had tossed her jacket over it. "Go shake hands with the devil, Stark. Like Delaney said, we McCalls stick together."

"And you?" he inquired of Brett.

Brittany McCall's answer was to the point, as always. "Maybe if you put a pork chop around your neck, marshal, you could at least get a dog to follow you."

Stark didn't flinch but his eyes revealed that her comment had hit home. He turned his gaze to Hank who sat silently on her cot, watching the proceedings with a cold, hard expression. "I think we all know that the ultimate decision rests in your hands, Miss Henrietta. So what are you going to do about it?"

"You're going to obscene measures to court my daughter," Luke cut in, looking desperate.

"The ante just went up, Luke. You know it goes deeper than that. I've given this a lot of thought, and I've decided I want payback for what you stole from me twenty-six years ago. I couldn't settle this matter with just a consent for courtship now. It would have to be more than that. We'll go straight to the marriage bed."

Luke's eyes turned murderous but he was as helpless as a cow in quicksand, and Stark knew it.

His top lip curled with amusement as he turned back to Hank. "I really think you ought to consider it, Miss Henrietta. If you consent, then you can feel good that you saved the lives of your family. I'm an important man in this town. You'd have all the security a woman wants and needs."

Hank finally lifted herself up off the cot and stood as toe to toe to Stark as the bars would allow. Her eyes chilled like a blue norther. "That's real encouraging to hear, Eli. A woman likes a sense of security." She saw the lustful, victorious gleam enter his eyes. "But frankly, I'd rather hang."

Stark's mood flashed to barely-contained rage. He stalked to the door and yanked his hat off its hook. "You'll come crawling before this is over, Hank McCall. You just wait and see."

He slammed the door behind him. Luke collapsed on his cot. "Damn it, Hank. You had me worried. I was afraid you were going to give in to him."

"Maybe I should, Dad, if it would get us out of here. I could always divorce him."

"Don't be foolish," Delaney said hotly. "Once he had you in his possession, he'd see you dead before he ever let you go."

Hank sat on the cot again and stared down at the floor. "You're probably right about that, Delaney, but it might be the only ace in the hole we're going to get. It's a chance I'll have to be willing to take."

Delaney awoke to the incessant sound of hammering and the strident call of the paperboy hollering, "Extra! Extra! Read all about it! Marshal Stark catches the McCall Gang red-handed!"

Delaney came off the cot so fast, she had to sit back down until the dizziness cleared from her head. But her voice worked fine and she hollered out for Hank and the twins and Daddy to wake up. Before they'd even cleared the sleepy-slivers from their eyes she was pacing the spot in front of her cot. "Since when did we become a gang? Stark! Get in here! You've got some explaining to do!"

Stark finally ambled in as if time meant nothing to him. He sipped at his coffee while Luke demanded an explanation. "Why did you take this to the newspaper, Stark? We're no gang and we're not horse thieves and you know it."

"This is going to ruin our reputation," Brett said angrily. "People are going to think we're a bunch of outlaws."

Stark enjoyed their predicament. "Some of those deputies with me yesterday must have leaked the arrest to the newspaper."

The paperboy had gone on down the street, hollering, "McCall Gang set to hang!"

Delaney paled. "Is that the hammering I hear?"

Stark gloated. "They figured they'd better get started on the gallows since the circuit judge will be around at the end of the week."

"We have a right to a trial, Stark."

"There's a public defender. He'll be in this afternoon, unless you've got your own lawyer you'd like to contact."

By then they'd all sat back down on their cots, realizing the enormity of what Stark's vendetta had turned into. He said that he'd bring them some breakfast from the restaurant across the street, just as soon as they had it prepared. Then he sauntered out, settled at his desk and proceeded to push some papers around.

Two hours later, they'd forced themselves to eat the fare from the restaurant—none of them had much of an appetite—and were just sliding their plates back under the bars when the young rancher, Bart Breckenridge, came in. He asked Stark for some privacy. The marshal, with a fresh cup of coffee in hand, obliged by settling himself in his slat-back rocker out on the boardwalk. But he left the door open and took the keys with him.

"Wouldn't want you to get some foolish notion to bust them out of here."

Bart looked like a longhorn bull on the prod. "You're the talk of the town, Luke," he said, keeping his voice low so Stark couldn't hear. "I was over to the cafe this morning and I overheard talk that Stark plans to hang you all, one at a time, starting with the youngest and leaving you until last so you can suffer your folly to the fullest."

"The off-handed stroke of a pen and we're outlaws." Andy looked like she might lose her breakfast.

Luke paced the confines of his small cell. "He's being damned presumptuous. We haven't even had the trial yet."

Bart glanced at Stark through the open door. He was smiling and greeting people as if it was the best day of his life. "Everybody is also saying that you don't have a chance of getting out of this," he said. "Nobody who knows you and your daughters believes the charges, but Stark has you cross-hobbled. What'd you do to get on his bad side anyway?"

Luke ran a weary hand through hair that needed a comb. "He was in love with the woman I married."

Breckenridge's brows arched. "So it's a sore that's had a good long time to fester?"

"You could say that."

"Maybe I shouldn't even suggest this, Luke, but we've seen Stark hang innocent men before on trumped-up charges just to satisfy personal vendettas." Breckenridge lowered his voice even more. "Maybe me and the boys could break you out of here."

Luke shook his head. "I'm not an outlaw and I don't want to be turned into one. I don't want my daughters spending the rest of their lives on the run. Besides, I'd hate to see you and your men implicated. You'd be running right alongside us."

"Only 'til I killed him." Breckenridge's jaw clenched; he wasn't joking. "You won't get any sympathy from old Judge Potter. Stark has him buffaloed into thinking he's an honest, upstanding citizen of the community, doing the best job ever of keeping the criminal element in hand. Stark'll win over the jury, too, either with bribes or threats against their families. One way or the other, he'll convince them that it's in their best interest to find you and your daughters guilty."

"There's a way out of this," Hank said, coming to the bars.

"You aren't going to do that." Luke glared at his oldest daughter.

"It beats hanging or running for the rest of our lives."

"Don't be so sure of that. Stark could make a woman wish she were dead."

"What is it, Miss McCall?" Bart asked anxiously, still believing he might find a way out for them.

Hank glanced at her dad, then turned her attention to Breckenridge. The latter's brown eyes had softened as they met hers. He was only a few years older than Hank and had never married. Hank sensed he liked her, but he was shy when it came to women. "He wants to marry me because I remind him of my mother," she said. "Daddy flatly told him no."

It took Breckenridge a minute to find his tongue. "That's what this is all about?" He shook his head in disbelief. "I've never heard of anything so preposterous."

"Nobody said he was running on a full load of coal," Delaney remarked.

Breckenridge agreed. "All the more reason that you break out of here and leave California. I could try to sort things out for you while you're gone. You wouldn't want marriage to Stark to even be a consideration, Miss McCall. Your father was right to turn him down."

Luke sat down on the edge of the cot. The reality of the situation was settling in hard. He and his daughters were going to hang if a miracle didn't take place. But he couldn't, in good faith and conscience, put Hank at Stark's mercy.

"I'd really like to see justice prevail, Bart," he said. "I keep holding out hope that it will when we can get up and tell our story at the trial."

"If you go through with a trial, it'd be too late to strike any bargains with him. Stark will make sure you're found guilty."

"Then I guess we'd have no choice at that point but to break out."

Bart shook his head. "By then he'd throw so many guards up around this place, you'd never be able to. Right now, he only has himself and a deputy. He must be thinking you're going to cave in to his demands."

"I'll just have to weigh things some more, Bart. See how things shape up as we get closer to the trial. Did you get those horses out at the blind corral?"

"We did, and we deposited the money in your bank account. Listen, Luke, there's a good lawyer in San Francisco by the name of William Proffit. I could send one of my men to get him. If you get one in this district, he's probably had a sit-down with Stark."

Hope flickered in Luke's eyes. "I'd be obliged, Bart."

"A fast-talking lawyer might be your only chance. I have a feeling this trial is going to boil down to your word against Stark's. We've all heard about that alleged bill of sale."

"Somebody ought to kill that sneaking coyote," Delaney commented from her cot. "And I'd like to be the one."

"You'd have to stand in line," Breckenridge said. Then, "My hands are tied, Luke, but my mouth isn't gagged. I'll be letting out the word to everybody in these parts how Stark is framing you and why. Sooner or later, people will grow a backbone and do something to stop him."

Stark moseyed inside. "Visitin' time's up, Breckenridge. You ought to mind who you keep company with anyway. Somebody might think you're part of their gang."

Breckenridge's lips pursed in disgust as he glared at Stark. "Gang, hell. Luke McCall and his daughters are honest people making an honest living. Somebody's gonna lay you low one of these days, you weasel. Hell, it might even be me."

Breckenridge said his farewells to the McCalls and stalked from the jail.

Stark stood in the doorway, watching Breckenridge ride from town. "Now, there's a man who thinks his money can keep him out of trouble," he said for the benefit of the McCalls. "That's what's wrong with people nowadays. They don't understand their position in life. They don't remember, until it's too late, that their lives are in the hands of those who hold the power."

CHAPTER FOUR

DODGING THE LOOP

Hank McCall had her back to the wall. She sat on her cot in the tiny cell she shared with Delaney and listened to her sister play every melancholy song she knew on her pocket harmonica. Delaney pretended to be preoccupied with the music, but every so often she would give Hank a look that said she knew exactly what was on Hank's mind. And she probably did, because there wasn't much that slipped past the youngest McCall. It didn't matter. Hank was the reason for them being in trouble, and she was going to have to be the one to find a way out of this loop they'd gotten themselves into.

Their father was asleep, lulled by Delaney's music. He hadn't slept more than a wink or two since this whole fiasco had started. Hank decided that locking him up was akin to corralling that yellow dun stallion; the confines were killing his soul.

Andy and Brett were engaged in a game of draw poker; Andy was winning. Andy had a way with cards that their daddy called "brilliant deduction." She could have sat down at a table with the smoothest-talking tinhorn around and drained his pockets of every last coin in no time at all. With her sweet smile, he probably wouldn't even mind.

It was no wonder Brett was losing. Her mind wasn't on the game. She was talking about that blue dress again and how she had wanted more than anything to stroll down the streets of Paris. How she'd have her hair professionally curled and pinned up under a feathered hat. How her hands would be covered in lace, not buckskin. And how she'd have a fancy parasol instead of the dusty brim of a man's hat to protect her fair complexion from the sun.

Hank's gaze shifted to Stark. He'd left the door open that separated the cells from his office. She decided he didn't look like a snake. If a body didn't know him, they might find him almost agreeable to the eye. He was reading the newspaper now that his paperwork was done. All he had left to do was wait for the trial day after tomorrow.

"If that defense lawyer they'd appointed us had been worth his salt," Andy said suddenly, as if she'd read Hank's mind, "you'd probably have gotten your wish, Brett."

Hank sighed and closed her eyes, remembering the defense attorney who had staggered in two days ago with Red Eye on his breath and a bowler on his head. He'd pulled up a chair in front of the bars and gone over the case with them. It had become apparent soon enough that he didn't believe their innocence. He was new to California, an Easterner who had come west to escape an arranged marriage. He'd looked down his nose at the five of them in their rough, soiled mustanging attire, then he'd left, telling them that he would see what he could do to "concoct" a defense.

They'd held out hope that the lawyer from San Francisco would show up, but Breckenridge had brought word just this morning that their last hope had a murder trial that was going to keep him busy for another week.

"I'll meet your bet and call you." Andy tossed some dry pinto beans into the center of the cot that was serving as a card table. Stark had only allowed them to use the beans after he had warily deduced that they could not use them as a means of escape.

Hank stared at the dirty ceiling. It was coated with a yellowish-brown stain, the onslaught of years of tobacco smoke.

They'd die for me. I can't let them do that. . . .

She broke out in a cold sweat, feeling like she might retch. Slowly she rose from the bed and went to the bars, leaning her burning face against the cool metal. There was really only one choice to make.

Delaney was playing her harmonica as if she were practicing for a funeral. Andy shuffled the cards for another game of poker. Brett sat cross-legged on the cot, still talking, and waiting patiently for her cards as if they had an infinity of tomorrows. Their father slept on.

This was as good a time as any.

"Hey, Stark. I need to go out back again." She spoke no louder than necessary to get his attention, lest she disrupt her father's slumber.

Stark looked up from his newspaper and saw that it was Hank calling. He laid the paper aside and unfolded himself from the chair.

"Been considering my proposal, Miss Henrietta?" He swaggered over to the bars.

His presumptuous air once again started a fire of rage in Hank's belly, but she would need the energy of that fire if she hoped to live through this battle. "I need an escort to the outhouse."

Disappointment fluttered in his eyes. "What a shame. I was really hoping you had come to your senses."

He opened the cell and Hank stepped through, glancing over her shoulder to make sure her father was still asleep and her sisters unsuspecting. Delaney was eyeing her, as if she might know what was running through her head, but she kept on with her music and said nothing.

Hank led the way quickly from the jailhouse along the hard packed path. Stark took his usual position on the stump that was located a dozen feet from the privy. He normally sat there and smoked while his prisoners took care of business, but this time Hank leaned a shoulder against the outhouse and said, "I'll see you dead, Stark, before I let you hang my family over this stupid vendetta of yours."

Her words threw him off guard for only a moment. "Well, you can't do that now, can you? Unless you've got some power that will just strike me dead. Like a bolt of lightning from the blue." He laughed at her, lifting his arm in a twisting motion simulating lightning. His sneering face was suddenly the ugliest sight she'd ever seen.

"No, I don't have that kind of power," she replied, "but I do have the power to turn this situation around. Drop the charges and I'll marry you."

His eyes lit up and he smiled leeringly. "I knew you'd come crawlin'."

"I'm still on my own two feet, marshal." She stifled the urge to spit in his face and call the whole thing off. But she couldn't. She had to think of her family.

He rose to his feet and sauntered over to her, his thumbs latched in his gun belt. He reminded her of a vulture, circling a dying man, relishing the prospect of picking out his eyes. Boldly he lifted a lock of hair from her shoulder and rubbed it caressingly between his fingers.

She said, "There is one condition, however."

He was amused. "You're not really in a bargaining position, Henrietta."

"I want papers. *Legal* papers that say the charges against us have been dropped. And I want your signature on them. Then I want five copies of the dismissal, one for each one of us."

"Why fool with all that, Henrietta? I can just turn the key in the lock and you'll all be free. End of matter."

"What's to keep you from double-crossing us again? No, Stark. That's the condition. Take it or leave it. And you say nothing to my father until it's all said and done."

He moved his hand from her hair to her cheek. It took all her willpower to keep from pulling away. "All right. Your family will be free by six o'clock tomorrow night, and you and I will be married shortly after."

"Aren't you even going to give me time to wash off the trail dirt and buy a dress? A woman wants to look good on her wedding day."

He rocked back on his heels, considering. Finally he said, "It'd be right nice to have you all sweet-smelling when I carry you over the threshold to my bed."

She could see his evil intentions reflected in his eyes. "Then it's done."

She slid out of his reach, fighting the urge to double over and empty her stomach right there on his boots. Instead, she stood tall as she returned to the jailhouse, holding onto a confident, arrogant strut. Eli Stark had not broken her or her family, and he never would. Nobody broke a McCall.

"You heard right, Dad." Hank forced herself to look into her father's disappointed eyes. "I'm getting you all out of here."

Luke McCall stood at the open cell door, as if he were going to refuse to go through it. "Marryin' this low-life son of a scorpion isn't the answer, Hank."

"I know what I'm doing. Trust me."

"Get on out of here, Luke," Stark commanded. "You're wasting time. Henrietta has to find herself a ready-made dress for the wedding this afternoon."

Brett sauntered over next to Hank. "What kind of a proper wedding dress can she get in that length of time, Stark?"

"If she can't buy one, I know lots of women in town who would loan her one. Besides, what she wears doesn't matter to me at all." His lecherous gaze slid over Hank from top to bottom. "She'll just be takin' it off real soon anyway."

"I'll see you dead—" Luke made a lunge for Stark, but Stark's pistol came up, gouging him in the ribs.

"Not if you're dead first, old pal."

"It's all right, Dad." Hank took his arm to restrain him. "Let's get going. There's a dress and millinery shop at the end of the street. Should I meet you at the courthouse, Stark?"

"I think you can call me Eli now, Henrietta." A sly smile creased his thin lips. "But I'll just mosey along with you."

"Afraid I'll keep going?"

"What's to stop you? You've got your walking papers in hand."

Hank had hoped he'd be fool enough to trust her. "All right, but we'll stop at the courthouse first. I want to make sure you conducted everything legally."

His eyes narrowed angrily. "I told you I did. Is this any way to start a marriage? Not trusting your husband's word?"

She shrugged. "You didn't trust mine. Besides, *Eli*, once a man lies, nobody ever believes him again."

Hank led the way to the courthouse, past the curious townspeople who had read all about their "rampage of horse stealing" in the newspaper. Some were whispering behind their hands, wondering why they were out on the street. Others who knew them were delighted to hear that the charges had been dropped, and they went off to spread the word. Of course, the newspaper would carry the full explanation of their release in tomorrow's paper. Hank wondered if any of the townspeople would believe the "lack of evidence" story that Stark had given the reporter, especially when there would probably also be an article about their marriage. But Stark's mind was twisted. He could convince himself that whatever he did could be explained away and people would be stupid enough to accept it.

At the courthouse, Hank found that Stark had indeed filed everything.

"Happy now?" he goaded. "I didn't just *say* I did it."

Hank once again led the way, this time out to the granite steps of the building. She stood on the top step and pulled her hat down onto her forehead. "Well, Daddy, sisters. I guess it's about time to hit the mustang trail again. What do you say we quit this town? I never liked Hawk's Point much even before this mess."

Her family was as tongue-tied as Stark, but the marshal recovered first. "What do you mean, leave this town? We had a deal."

"Now, isn't that funny? If I recall we had a deal on those mustangs, too. I guess a person's word just isn't worth a tinker's damn these days, is it?" She shrugged then started down the steps. The others followed, grinning from ear to ear.

"I'll get you for this, Hank McCall. Why, you're nothing but a two-bit whore."

She stopped at the bottom of the steps and looked up at him. "Don't try causing us any grief, Stark, or I'll put you to bed permanently."

Then she strolled away, leaving him boiling in his own stew.

CHAPTER FIVE

LOOSE CINCH

The McCalls weren't known for double-crossing, lying, or going back on their word, but they weren't above getting even. There was a time for pulling a card out of your sleeve, and a time to just play the hand you were dealt. Nobody held it against Hank for doing the former. One thing was certain, the McCalls wouldn't be victims *or* martyrs. With that sour affair behind them, they headed home to Monterey. The girls were looking forward to a romp on the beach.

Luke McCall had built his and Melinda's little *cabaña* on a cliff overlooking an isolated cove, protected from the wind that came up off the ocean.

Things had changed a lot in California in the past twenty-five years, mostly due to the discovery of gold fifteen years before, but the majority of the Forty-Niners who had come to California seeking their fortunes had gone inland via San Francisco and Sacramento. The *cabaña* still stood alone with gnarled cypresses and other trees and brush surrounding it on three sides. Its front faced the ocean, and a well-traveled path switch-backed through foliage to the water below. The thousand acres that the *cabaña* was situated on helped to maintain privacy.

Luke stood on the cliff, hands in his pockets, and watched his daughters romping in the surf, soaking the swimming dresses they'd diligently sewn several years ago. He recalled the times in his own youth when he'd walked on the sand, hand in hand with Melinda. They'd been so young and carefree. They'd run out into the water up to their waists, laughing as the surf came in. They'd made love afterwards on a blanket just below the cliff.

After Melinda had died, he had never walked the beach again. From then on, Hank had been the one to take the younger girls down and watch them while they played in the sand. It had been too much responsibility for a child. He could see that now.

"Hey, Daddy!" Delaney called through cupped hands. "Come on down and get your feet wet!"

The others motioned, calling out and encouraging him. He'd always just laughed and told them he didn't like getting wet, so they were surprised when he suddenly took the winding trail that led to the beach below.

He stopped where the girls had a pile of towels and paraphernalia piled on the sand. He dropped to his fanny and yanked off his boots and socks then peeled out of his shirt. Squealing with delight, the twins each grabbed one of this hands. With Hank and Delaney pushing him along, he ran into the water, laughing, before he changed his mind.

"I'm a female, Delaney, and—unlike you—I don't feel short-changed by it at all." Brett was stretched out on a blanket on the sand beneath an umbrella, wearing next to nothing and soaking up the warmth of the sun. With the gilt-edged mirror in hand, she was again plucking at her unruly dark eyebrows.

"Daddy needs our help, Brett," Delaney argued from her blanket, watching a flock of seagulls squawking overhead. "You can't run out on him. We're a family and families should stick together. If even one of us leaves, it would break

58

the core, and nothing would ever be the same again."

They could only talk about their father now because he was up at the *cabaña,* napping in the shade. They'd worn him out with all the surf-wrestling and swimming they'd done earlier.

"We can't mustang for the rest of our lives, Delaney."

"I don't see why not."

Brett lowered the mirror and slashed Delaney with impatient blue eyes. "I can just see the four of us, gray hair streaming, brittle bones creaking, riding hell-bent after wild horses. It's not practical, Delaney. Back me up on this, Hank."

Hank opened groggy eyes at the sound of her name. She rolled from her stomach to her back and asked Brett to repeat the question. After a moment of contemplation, she said, "There are days when I can't see myself doing anything else. Days when settling down to a husband and children and giving up my freedom is the last thing I want to do. Other times I'd like to have my own home and family. So I guess I'll just keep on doing what I'm doing until something comes along to change my life." Suddenly she grinned. "Like meeting a man who falls head over heels in love with me."

"I think there already is one." Andy grinned slyly.

Hank's interest was piqued. "Who?"

"Bart Breckenridge. When he's around, he sees only you. I thought he was going to scoop you up and hug you when we stopped by his place on the way home."

"He was just happy to see we'd worked our way out of Stark's rope," Hank insisted. "That's all."

"Oh, I don't think so," Andy teased knowingly. "I wouldn't be surprised at all to see him get the courage to come courting now that he realizes he just about lost you."

"He *is* handsome," Hank conceded.

Delaney clicked her tongue in annoyance. "Romance and men. That's all you three want to talk about when there are bigger concerns in life, like Stark turning us into horse thieves. That'll be a black mark that will follow us around for the rest of our lives. Mark my word, every time a horse comes up missing around here, people will accuse the McCalls."

"I think people know better," Hank said on a positive note.

"Well, what about you?" Delaney turned to Andy. "You can't possibly think cooking and cleaning and diaper-changing would be any way to live. Why, I'd almost rather be an outlaw!"

Andy sat up from where she'd been lying on her stomach, watching the rise and fall of the surf as it crept higher onto the sand. "I can't say I'm feeling overly anxious to get married, even if I am twenty-two. There's a few things I'd like to do first and I haven't seen one man I'd want to marry."

"What are some of the things you want to do?"

Andy exchanged a glance with Brett, one of those looks that said they had a secret. It wasn't surprising. They always had secrets. "Should I tell them, sis?"

Brett seemed apprehensive for a moment but finally shrugged. "I guess it doesn't matter, but just don't tell Daddy. He'd probably think it was a crazy notion and try to talk us out of it."

Delaney feigned indifference. "Well, whatever it is, I'd wager twenty broomtails that you won't have the nerve to do it anyway."

Andy ignored her. "Will you and Hank keep it a secret?"

Hank sat up, drawing her knees to her chest and circling them with her arms. "There's a lot of things Daddy doesn't know about us girls. I don't suppose one more will matter."

"All right," Delaney agreed. "I'll keep quiet."

Andy took a deep breath, mustering her courage. "The fact is, Brett and I want our own hotel. We've been talking about going into business for a long time now. It would be a luxurious establishment complete with marble-topped dressers, walnut beds, imported rugs, Nottingham lace curtains on gilt rods, and hydraulic elevators. It's just the sort of thing Monterey needs."

Delaney was amused. "And where do you think you'll get the money to build such a palace?"

"Brett and I are saving our money, and we figure we might be able to get some financial backing if we have a down payment."

"You might be saving yours, Andy, but Brett appears to have other plans for hers, like parasols and blue silk dresses."

Brett lowered the tweezers long enough to say, "I might have known you'd find some way to make fun of our plans."

"No bank is going to loan two single women enough money to build a hotel."

"Maybe not, but banks aren't the only ones with money. There are rich men around who wouldn't mind considering an investment with enterprising women."

"And I can tell you what they'd want for collateral."

"At least we have our sights set on something besides a broomtail's behind, which is more than I can say for you."

"I'm saving my money, too, but for more important things than gilt-edged mirrors and lace gloves that would fall apart if you looked crosswise at them."

"Well, the way you're going, you'll be needing to give all your money to Doc Tibbits because he's going to have one dickens of a time removing my boot from up your—"

Suddenly three shots rang out almost simultaneously from

61

the *cabaña*. All four girls leaped to their feet. Two more shots sounded, then another three.

"That can't be Daddy," Hank said, listening with growing concern. "Besides, he wouldn't have had time to reload. Somebody's up there."

More shots popped in the woods.

"What are we going to do? We don't even have a gun!"

"I do." Delaney was already digging through her bag. In an instant she had her six-shooter in hand.

Following her, they ran across the sand, bare feet flying, and started up the cliff path.

"Stay down," Hank called from behind Delaney. "We can't help him if we get ourselves killed."

Delaney kept scrambling up over the steep, packed path, using her free hand to grab rocks and bushes as she propelled herself to the top. More shots rang out, then shouts.

"He's inside with the women! We've got them now!"

Delaney stopped just feet from the top. She looked down at her sisters, stalled on the path behind her. Their frightened faces were reflections of her own. "My lord, somebody wants us all dead."

"Can you see who it is?"

Delaney moved up another couple of feet until she could peer over the lip of the trail to level ground. "I see two, moving in front of the house. Probably trying to keep Daddy from escaping out the front. There's two more covering the back. I can't see any others."

"And here we are barefoot with one gun and six bullets," Brett said. "If you start firing, Delaney, they'll be on us in an instant."

More shots were fired at the *cabaña*. The girls listened to see where they were coming from, deducing there were no more than the four assailants Delaney had seen.

"We'll burn 'em out!" one man shouted from the side of the house.

Delaney's eyes locked with Hank's. "They've got Daddy surrounded. I've got no choice but to move and try to kill them."

"Why do they want to kill us?" Andy voiced from below.

"The only person I know of that would want us dead is Stark, but he's not one of them. At least, not that I can tell."

Hank grabbed Delaney's ankle as she started up the path again. "I'll go."

"We both know I can knock a squirrel's head off at fifty yards with one shot. And we both know you can't."

"Damn it, Delaney."

"Daddy hates it when you use profanity, Hank. Now, don't worry. I know these woods. I'll sneak up behind those two over there. I can get them both before they know what's happened. Then . . . well, I'll have to dive for cover and see what happens."

"You might be a good shot, little sister, but your strategy leaves something to be desired. I'm going with you."

"What have you got in mind?"

"Keeping you from getting killed. And if I can't do that, then I can always take over." She said it with a half smile but her eyes were dead serious.

"Brett and I can try to sneak into the house from the side door," Andy said. "We can help Daddy from the inside."

"No, that's too dangerous," Hank replied. "Stay put and see if we can even the odds."

Delaney was ready to move into the woods when one of their father's assailants popped up from out of his hiding place and threw off a shot at the *cabaña,* shattering a window. All was quiet from inside, no corresponding gunshots. The girls immediately feared that the bullet had found their father.

With Hank behind her, Delaney darted for the woods and melted into the protection of the timber and brush, all the while hoping the assailants wouldn't see the flashes of white from their swimming dresses. For the first time in her life, Delaney knew the true meaning of fear. But she couldn't think of the consequences. They had to save Daddy.

Anger and adrenaline propelled her forward quietly through the brush as she ignored the sticks and rocks gouging her bare feet. She circled wide to make sure she was behind the attackers and not between them and the house. She halted in some brush and peered through the branches. Hank slid into position next to her.

They sized up the situation for a moment or two, then Hank said, "Do you see that rock over there?"

Delaney spotted a boulder about twelve inches in diameter, ragged at the edges. "What's on your mind, Hank?"

"I'll sneak up on that guy to our right. With you as backup, I'll lay him low with the rock, take his gun. Then we'll move on to the next one, over there by the swing tree."

Delaney figured it was pretty risky, but they didn't have time to come up with alternatives. One man was hollering, "You'd better come out, McCall, or we're going to fire the place!"

Still no reply. Delaney nervously licked her lips and nodded. "All right. Let's move."

Hank gathered up the boulder, struggling with its weight. With difficulty she crept through the trees and undergrowth, advancing on the assailant, setting her bare feet down carefully with each step as soundless as a ghost. Her arm muscles began to ache and quiver from the burden of the boulder. Delaney was close behind, barely breathing, wondering if the knocking of her heart would be heard before her footsteps.

They stopped just six feet behind the gunman. As Hank

rose to her full height her knee joint popped. The gunman whirled. The boulder flew forward with a direct hit to his head. Blood spurted from his nose and mouth and he hit the ground with a thud. The girls dropped from sight behind the brush. The skirmish was covered by more gunshots and hollering.

"Come out with your hands up, McCall! You're surrounded and don't have a chance of escape!"

Delaney and Hank began stripping the gunman of his sidearm, gun belt, vest and shirt. Then they rolled him to his stomach and used the sleeves of the shirt to tie his hands behind his back. Hank tore a flounce off her swim dress and gagged him.

"I think he's dead," Delaney said.

"We can't take the chance. He might only be unconscious."

Hank strapped the gun belt around her narrow waist, reloaded the six-shooter, and replaced it in the holster. She gathered up the blood-smeared boulder. "Would you look at this. That guy's face didn't damage this rock at all. I say we use it again."

"Sounds like a fine idea to me."

In similar fashion, they managed to lay low another assailant, but then one of the enemies threw something inside the broken window and smoke came boiling out.

"They're burning the house," Delaney whispered frantically. "If Daddy comes out, they'll kill him."

Hank cast off the boulder and pulled out the six-shooter. "I guess that ends the subtleties. Let's start the second line of this siege. I'll take the one on the right. You take the one on the left."

"The curtains are on fire, Hank."

"Then it's now or never. Ready? One . . . two . . . three . . . FIRE!"

Bullets rained down on the assailants' nests. They started hollering in confusion and tried to bolt. A .44 slug winged one before the other yelled, "Let's get out of here!"

They fled for their horses, hidden somewhere in the trees. Hank and Delaney kept the bullets on their heels until they were out of sight. With guns still drawn and ready, they ran for the house. The flames licked up the sides of the window frame. By the time they burst through the door, their father was leaning against the wall with an empty water bucket dangling from his hand and his six-shooter aimed at them. The curtains were nothing but black, smoldering rags in the center of the tile floor.

"Daddy, are you all right?"

Luke McCall nodded and lowered his gun.

Delaney suddenly felt as limp as a neck-wrung rooster and collapsed in the closest chair. "Two got away, Daddy, but we got the other two. They may or may not be dead, but they're trussed up like Thanksgiving turkeys."

Luke McCall set the empty water bucket on the table. "Thanks, girls. Let's go take a look."

CHAPTER SIX

JUMPING FENCES

Luke turned the attackers onto their backs and the McCalls found out that Hank was only a murderer once over. The one that wasn't dead opened his eyes to a humdinger of a headache and swollen lips. He was missing several teeth, too, but he could still talk, and talk came easy when Luke pulled back the hammer on his long-necked Walker and said, "I'm only going to give you one chance to speak, pardner, so I suggest you put those jaws into motion and tell us just who you are and why you and your friends tried to kill us."

The stranger's Adam's apple bobbed as if he had a chunk of rotten meat passing through his gullet. He cowered on the ground with his back pressed tight to a tree. "Don't kill me, McCall. It ain't nothin' personal. My name's Jasper Bell. The sheriff at Hawk's Point deputized me and the others and told us to bring you in. Said he'd give us a special reward of five hundred dollars each, but he only gave us a couple of days to do it. If we didn't get you all back in custody by day after tomorrow, then he said he was going to print up a bunch of Wanted posters and send them all over California. He didn't really want to send out bounty hunters because he wanted that Hank girl alive and he figured bounty hunters wouldn't be too particular."

"Eli Stark put out a reward on us?" Hank's voice lifted shrilly.

"Yes, ma'am." His eyes darted nervously. "He had that

Eastern lawyer draw up a Wanted poster—the man professes to be an artist too, I guess. Then he took it over to the newspaper office and had a few printed up. I've got it right here in my vest pocket. See for yourself."

Jasper Bell looked genuinely frightened as Hank went for the poster. He probably figured she might come at him with another boulder.

The others gathered around as she warily unfolded the paper. The amateurish artist's renditions of their faces crowded the perimeters of the poster. Down the center, words in bold black letters leaped out at them:

$1000 REWARD

for

LUKE MCCALL

and his

FOUR DAUGHTERS

for the crimes of

MURDER, HORSE STEALING, JAIL BREAK

I will award $1000 to the man who can bring in all five of the McCalls, dead or alive, or $250 for each brought in separately. They are armed and dangerous.

Sheriff Elias J. Stark
Hawk's Point, California
County of Merced

Delaney blew up like a keg of dynamite. "Why that double-dealing jackal! We didn't do any of these things!"

Luke grabbed Bell by the shirtfront and hauled him to his feet. "What's this all about? We've murdered no one."

68

"What do you call that?" The man nodded toward his partner over in the brush.

"Protecting our property, you little weasel. Now whose murder are we being accused of?" Luke demanded, pressing his Walker Colt into Bell's face again.

Bell suddenly looked like he was going to soil his drawers, and the words came spurting out of him. "Stark's deputy was found with a bullet in his head out by the outhouse. Stark said one of those twins flirted with him out there and got the jump on him. Killed him."

"Aren't we clever?" Brett commented dryly, glancing at Andy. "Stark probably killed the man himself to trump up the charges and make it look like we did it during an escape."

"Yes, and afterward we just walked down to the courthouse—with Stark—in plain view of everyone," Andy said facetiously.

"Stark said he was your prisoner and that he had no choice but to go along with you," Jasper hastily explained. "All I know for certain is that word is spreading fast about the McCall gang, and every bounty hunter in the country will be on your trail as soon as those reward posters hit the street."

Hank leaned against a tree trunk and looked sick. "I'll go back and marry the lily-livered mongrel if that's what this is all about."

Luke's eyes sparked with alarm. "Stark isn't a man who likes to be bested, and that's what you did, Hank. Marrying him now will only give him encouragement to abuse his power even more . . . and that abuse will be directed towards you. He'll make you pay."

"He won't live long enough to exact a dime from me," she promised, with a hard set to her jaw. "If I'm going to hang for murder, then I might as well be guilty, and I'll start with him."

Luke searched for a better way. "We'll go to Monterey and talk to Sheriff Harley. We'll take Mr. Jasper Bell here along too and see if we can get to the bottom of this."

"You'd better watch your back, McCall," Bell ventured. "I've got two more buddies who'll be back to finish the job and do their collectin'. They don't care if you're guilty or not."

Luke gave Bell a shove toward the house. "No, I and don't suppose they'll care if you're dead or not either."

They waited until dusk then angled their way down to the beach. They had tied the dead man belly down on the horse they'd found tethered in the woods. By moonlight, with the surf slapping not far away, they covered the ten miles to Monterey in a little over an hour and rode in the back way. No sense in announcing their arrival by taking the middle of main street.

Sheriff Harley was still on duty, having just completed his rounds. Round-faced and barrel-chested, the forty-six-year-old sheriff sported a highly waxed, handlebar moustache, and was never seen in any attire except a three-piece suit and tie. He didn't reach five-foot-six, but it was remarked around town that he was an expert at the laws of leverage. He acquired the illusion of height by pushing the crown of his hat upward, eliminating all creases, and by wearing high-heeled boots. He rode a horse that was sixteen hands, and he packed an old Texas Paterson five-shot revolver whose twelve-inch barrel reached nearly to his knee. His fingers looked like link sausages, but didn't slow down his draw. Some called him the Napoleon of Monterey, but never to his face.

Luke McCall pushed Bell inside the sheriff's office. The girls hastily followed, promptly closing and locking the door behind them. Delaney and Andy went directly to the blinds and pulled them down.

Sheriff Harley seldom let anything ruffle his feathers, and this unusual visit was no exception. "From the looks of this man's face, Luke, I would hate to see your knuckles."

"His face met up with a boulder."

"Ah . . . well, that explains it then." With hands draped on his hips, Harley glanced over at the girls. "Ladies. There's hot water on the potbelly and a box of tea on the shelf. You're welcome to fix a pot if you've a mind. I like a good cup of tea myself on occasion so I always keep some on hand. Coffee's made, too. Get yourself a cup, Luke."

"Obliged, Harley."

The sheriff took Jasper Bell by the arm and led him into another part of the jail where there were two cells and a door dividing it from the main office.

"I ain't done nothing wrong!" Bell cried out, struggling for his freedom. "They're the ones who have a price on their heads. I'm a deputy marshal from Hawk's Point. Can't you see my badge?"

"I'm not locking you up permanently, sir. Just giving you a chance to take a load off your feet until I hear the grievance here from Luke. You have to understand, I've known Luke all my life and I don't know you from beans. Who's to say that star on your chest hasn't been stolen from some lawman you killed."

When Bell was secure, Harley sauntered back to his desk. He left the door open between his office and jail so Bell could hear what was said and comment if it suited him. Harley could never be accused of being unfair. His demeanor was nonchalant, but nothing escaped him. Those who underestimated Harley were those who didn't know him. Beneath his finely tailored clothes, his muscles were bunched and ready for action. So was his brain.

Luke had poured two cups of coffee and he handed one to

Harley. "This man and three others tried to kill me and my daughters out at our place. One of them was killed in the scuffle. His body's out back, draped over a horse. The other two got away. Bell says Sheriff Eli Stark up at Hawk's Point deputized him and three others and even offered them a reward to bring us in."

Harley sipped his coffee as if they were discussing the weather. After a minute he said, "Does this have anything to do with that charge of horse stealing up in Merced county?"

"I suspect it does."

"I thought that charge was dropped."

"So did we." Luke pulled out the Wanted poster and handed it to Harley, hoping his old friend wouldn't be honor bound to arrest them. He explained what Bell had told them.

The sheriff looked the poster over and let out a low whistle. "What'd you do to get on Stark's bad side?"

Hank stepped forward. "I refused an offer of marriage."

Harley's brows lifted. "Now, that's what I call a sore loser."

"It actually started twenty-five years ago," Luke said, and briefly explained the rivalry between him and Stark over Melinda. "What can we do to get him off our back, Harley?"

The sheriff's lips compressed; his brow furrowed. "I've had occasion to deal with Stark, and I'm aware that he doesn't see things in the same light as the rest of us."

"Will we have to go to trial to prove our innocence? If we do, we figure Stark will pay off the jury and the judge both and trump up the evidence. Unless we can get a change of venue."

"I've heard he's done that, Luke, but nobody has attempted to prove it. However, I just might be able to convince Stark to dismiss the charges—for good—if he wants to retain his position as marshal of Hawk's Point." He handed the poster back to Luke. "Pretend I never saw this."

"Obliged, Harley." Luke folded it back up and returned it to his pocket. "These posters, according to Bell, are going to be distributed to bounty hunters in a couple of days, if they haven't already. If that happens, my daughters and I will be hunted."

Harley puzzled over the situation for a time and finally found a viable course to take. "If I can't get Stark to back down from the charges, I might have to contact the U.S. Marshal. In the meantime, find a place to disappear until I get back. And don't go back to your ranch except to get clothes and supplies. If he's already leaked it to any bounty hunters, that's the first place they'll look. Meet me back here a week from tonight, at midnight. I hope I'll have Stark's badge by then."

Sam Saxton brushed a finger across the bloody boulder. The McCalls had been gone long enough for the blood to dry. On his haunches, he surveyed the skirmish that had taken place in the woods, the broken twigs and branches, the disrupted soil, the footprints—small and without shoes. Undoubtedly female. He found the spot in the trees where horses had been tied, but then saw where two of them had left in a hurry.

He smiled wryly. "It looks like those girls lobbed a counter attack," he murmured to himself. "Never underestimate the power of a woman. . . ."

He rose and picked his way carefully over to the empty *cabaña*. Bullets had chipped and lodged in the adobe and wood. The siege against the McCalls had been a healthy one, probably with four or more lawmen, or bounty hunters, involved. He liked a good fight, but this one should never have taken place. Stark had hired *him* to bring in the McCalls.

Now, from all appearances, Stark had double-crossed him and sent others. For that, the oily marshal would pay.

Inside the *cabaña*, the only disruption was burned curtains. No blood or sign of a scuffle. That alone told him that the bounty hunters hadn't made it inside the house and hadn't wounded any of the McCalls who might have been in here. From the pattern of ammunition on the floor, he figured only one McCall—probably the father—had been in the house, firing from the broken window. The tracks outside indicated that the girls had scrambled up the beach path, probably when they'd heard gunshots.

What he couldn't tell from the sign was where the McCalls had gone. By surveying the three bedrooms and the pantry, he concluded that they hadn't packed anything when they'd left, so it was likely they'd be back.

He sauntered into the parlor and nosed around. He found an old daguerreotype of a woman he surmised was the mother of the girls. The photo looked to be about twenty-five or thirty years old. Next to it was a more recent photograph of Luke McCall and his four grown daughters. All were dressed in their Sunday best. McCall was a tall, handsome man, and his daughters were undeniably beautiful. But they didn't look like killers or thieves. In fact, you wouldn't know from looking at them that they'd been raised on the wild side. It was a pity he was going to have to bring them in so they could hang. Such a waste.

Settling into Luke McCall's easy chair with the photograph in his lap, Sam Saxton lit a cheroot. The only sound was the ticking of a grandfather clock in the corner. Blowing smoke to the ceiling, he absorbed the simple comforts of the unpretentious *cabaña*. It was a place that made him feel right at home. Maybe after the McCalls were hanged he'd have a try at laying claim to it. He'd been having a hankering lately to get a ranch, settle down.

With dusk descending, he lit a hurricane lamp and continued to study the photograph of Luke McCall and his daughters. He pulled the Wanted poster from his shirt pocket and spread it out on his knee. The hand-drawn images held no resemblance whatsoever to the actual people. If a body hadn't seen them firsthand, they'd never recognize them from this pathetic artist's interpretation, which was fine. If there were others out there searching for them, they'd be less likely to find them.

Suddenly a noise from outside sent him melting into the shadows. If the McCalls had returned, they'd see the light and know there was a stranger in the house. If it was those ambushers returning, they might think *he* was McCall. Whoever it was, they'd be gunning for him.

Saxton had learned that all things come to the man who is willing to wait, and he did not have to wait long. He suspected that whoever was out there would try to sneak in through the door that faced the ocean since it was clearly used less often than the other.

Shortly the latch twisted and ever-so-slowly the door moved inward. Two men eased their way into the parlor and toward McCall's chair that had its back to them. They lifted their six-shooters and were taking aim, thinking someone was in the chair, when Saxton growled in a low voice, "You boys lookin' for someone?"

They whirled. Saxton's bullets threw them backwards, one onto the hardwood floor, the other onto the rug.

Sam left the shadow by the grandfather clock and rolled the one off the rug. He didn't want them to bleed all over it. He'd gotten them dead-center. It eased his conscience to know he hadn't killed anybody that didn't deserve it. They might be in the same profession as he was, but he held no illusion to the type of men they were.

He took a minute to feel around their pockets and found what he was looking for: the reward poster. It was the same one that Stark had given to him, supposedly exclusively. There was no doubt about it now. The marshal had some explaining to do.

He snuffed out the lantern, slipped outside and took a surveillance. He found only two horses tied in the trees. Feeling confident that he was alone, he draped the bodies over the two horses and tied them down. He'd missed his chance at the McCalls, thanks to these reprobates, but he'd make sure there was no more interference in the future.

Delaney knew someone had been in the house the minute she stepped over the threshold. She stopped dead in her tracks, nostrils flaring. "That isn't your tobacco, Daddy."

The others tried to pick up the scent. Andy and their father finally admitted they noticed something faintly different about the aroma.

"Somebody's been in here all right," Luke said, calmly palming his Walker. "And they still might be. Stark could have released those posters as easily as not and lied to Bell about it."

They'd ridden home in the dark and the sun was still an hour from rising. There were any number of shadows where an intruder could be hiding. Andy and Hank lit two lamps. Luke led the search for the intruder, but the lamps illuminated only an empty house virtually undisturbed, except for the stub of a cheroot in Luke McCall's ash tray.

"Gutsy, I'd say." Brett fingered the stub. "The brazen dog must have sat right here in Daddy's chair."

"Yes, and look here." Delaney stood in front of the fireplace with her hands on her hips, a cold chill settling over her.

76

"The photograph of us and Daddy is missing from the mantle."

That unsettled them all. It was bad enough to know that they had been targets of assassins and had had their home invaded. To have the precious photograph stolen was worse. Whoever had stolen it knew exactly what they looked like now.

"He must have figured we'd already high-tailed it out of here," Hank said. "We'd better get gone before he discovers the truth."

They dispersed, packing personal items and clothing to last a week. While the girls put together supplies, their father went to the pasture and caught two pack horses. They had everything loaded by the time the sun had cleared the treetops. Still, they were more reluctant to leave than they ever had been when they'd gone for weeks to mustang. There was something different about closing the door on a house that they might never see again.

Luke McCall stood in the doorway, wondering if bounty hunters would come in and strip the place while they were gone. "You girls get mounted," he said. "And keep an eye out. There could be more of 'em out there."

He waited until they'd all left the house, then he walked to the mantle and tucked the daguerreotype of Melinda inside his shirt.

Sam Saxton trotted the horses into Hawk's Point, ignoring the curious stares of the townspeople as they observed the two dead bodies belly-down in their saddles. He pulled rein in front of the jailhouse and stepped to the ground. Securing the horses at the hitching rail, he strode inside. Stark was at his mahogany desk, playing solitaire. His initial surprise at seeing Sam was quickly chased by wariness. He looked past him, through the open door, as if expecting to see someone else.

"I didn't expect you to come back empty-handed, Saxton."

"I didn't." Saxton stopped just inside the door, taking a careless stance with thumbs looped in his gun belt.

Stark's eyes shifted to the door again. He finally pushed himself out of the chair and clomped over to the window. He saw the dead bodies and smiled. "Good. Two down, two to go. Which ones did you get?" He shoved past Saxton to see for himself.

Saxton sauntered to the door and leaned against the frame, watching Stark. The marshal lifted the head of the first body. A startled gasp roared up his throat. "This isn't one of the McCalls, you idiot! This is my deputy!"

"We had a deal, Stark." Saxton pulled the Wanted poster from his pocket and unfolded it with purposeful intent. "You asked me to collect this wild bunch and you said you'd pay me a thousand dollars if I brought them in, dead or alive, preferably dead—all except the one named Hank. Is that correct?"

"Yes, but that doesn't explain why you killed my deputy."

Saxton was indifferent. "They mistook me for Luke McCall. It was a clear-cut thing. I could have handed the McCalls over to you by now. You said you wouldn't print and distribute any more of the posters until you gave me a week. Is that correct?"

Stark shifted uneasily; his eyes darkened warily. "Make your point, Saxton."

"This Wanted poster was not the one you gave me. It was on your deputy." He saw the redness creeping into Stark's face. "They were after the McCalls, too, but they found me instead. Now, you explain why they were down there, Stark, when you gave *me* the contract."

"I didn't send them, if that's what you're thinking. The deputy must have gotten hold of one of the other posters. He must have stolen it and acted on his own."

"Did he know about the deal I had with you?"

"Listen, Saxton. I'm sorry he stepped on your toes, but I'm not his keeper. How am I going to explain his death to his wife and the town?"

"Tell them he went after the McCalls; he got the short end of the stick. It shouldn't make any difference. They're going to hang for one murder, they might as well hang for three.

"Now, I'm only going to say this once, Stark, so listen, and listen real good. I don't know how many more you've sicced on the McCalls, but you'd be wise to call 'em off or I'll be coming after *you*. I don't like double-crossers."

Stark's lip curled derisively, but Saxton saw it quivering ever-so-slightly. "With me dead, you won't get your reward money."

"Sometimes there's more satisfaction in killing than receiving." He shoved past Stark but the marshal's voice stopped him.

"Do you have any idea where the McCalls are?"

Saxton eyed Stark with thinning patience. He didn't like the man, hadn't right from the beginning. He knew that Stark had a bad tendency of playing both sides of the law. He had no tolerance for that. He'd wondered why there were so many people fooled by Stark that they kept re-electing him. Didn't anybody dare run against him?

As for himself, there had been few times in his life when he hadn't looked a man—or a woman—in the eyes and known inherently the true nature of their souls.

"Tracks were everywhere," he finally replied, "thanks to these two. Indications were that there were also two more. I figure the McCalls got them. As for your horse thieves, they could have gone in any direction, even West if they had a boat."

"We can always end this contract here and now, Saxton. I only contacted you because I heard you were the best tracker in these parts."

"I'm flattered. I'll keep looking for the McCalls, but it'll be tougher now to find them. Could take me a lot longer to get a lead and find a way to bring them in."

"How hard can it be to put a bullet in them?"

"I don't like cold-blooded killing, Stark. Besides, if gunfire breaks out, you don't want me to accidentally kill the one you want, do you?"

"How much longer?"

He shrugged noncommittally. "Weeks. Maybe even months. Your deputy and his cronies just made my job a sight harder. The McCalls have taken to the willows. If I'm going to continue, I'm going to need a bigger retainer—say five hundred—and you'll have to raise the ante to two thousand."

"Pretty proud of yourself, aren't you? I can just send out these posters and every bounty hunter in California will be after them."

Saxton gathered his reins and swung into the saddle. "Sounds as if you already have. But suit yourself. You send out more bounty hunters and those McCalls will all come back draped over the saddle just like your deputy. That woman you're lusting after won't be too fun to bed down with if she's staring at the sky and seeing nothing." He started to rein away from the hitching rail but Stark called him back.

"All right, Saxton. I'm going to give you a month, but no more, then I open the floodgates."

"Five hundred, Stark. Traveling expenses. And just remember how bad you want that woman in one piece. Two months or nothing."

Stark glared but went inside, fiddled around in front of his safe, then came out with five hundred in cash. "I'm going to want something for that, Saxton."

"Namely?"

"Luke McCall dead. The others you can bring in alive."

"McCall will be the easy one."

"How do you figure? The others are women, for cryin' out loud."

Saxton smiled but it was without humor. "It could be harder to bring in the women."

"How so?"

"Because Luke McCall's daughters are awfully pretty ladies, and I have a weakness for ladies. I might just want to sample the wares a little before I turn them over to you."

"How long does it take you to sample the wares?"

"When a man is out to get the best music from a violin he doesn't treat it like a fiddle. I guess you wouldn't know anything about music."

Stark stood in helpless fury as Saxton kicked his bay into a lope. That high-handed bounty hunter didn't have a thread of moral decency. If he thought he was going to get his two thousand dollars and use Hank for his own pleasures in the process, he was dead wrong. Stark had an ace in the hole. That was one thing he always made sure of.

CHAPTER SEVEN

CROW-HOPPING

Delaney looked at the Wanted poster for a long while, trying to see a resemblance to her and her family in the sorry sketches. She wondered if Stark himself had taken ink to paper and tried to draw their likenesses.

"I flat object to these drawings," she finally voiced her disgruntlement. "This is an insult to Mama and Daddy both. If we all really looked this dog-ugly, why, it'd be merciful to society if we'd just go hang ourselves."

The campfire burned brightly between the McCalls. They had wearily eaten a meal of chipped beef, soda biscuits, and coffee. Beyond the fire, Carmel Valley was lost to the darkness, but the mountains on either side were sharply illuminated by stars in a cloudless sky. They had been hiding out two days' ride from Monterey and had pitched a couple of tents in the trees. It was a place they'd camped often while mustanging.

"You've been harboring resentment towards those sketches for five days now," Brett snapped. She was clearly getting antsy and ready to move on. "You ought to be glad they don't look like us. Maybe we'll be less recognizable to all the bloodhounds who are probably on our trail even as we speak."

Andy tried to ease the tension. "Any bounty hunter who sees or hears of a man riding with four women is going to ignore likenesses and make deductions."

Hank prodded the fire with a stick. "I'm wondering if we ought to split up."

Delaney studied her oldest sister in the glow of the firelight. Hank looked like she'd aged ten years in the past five days, and Delaney didn't believe it had anything to do with the hard riding. They were all accustomed to days in the saddle so Delaney knew those haggard lines around Hank's mouth and eyes were due to the worry and guilt gnawing at her insides.

"We're family," Delaney asserted, almost belligerently. "Family sticks together. Besides, if we split up, we're even more vulnerable. Isn't that what you've always told us, Daddy?"

Luke McCall stared over the rim of his coffee cup into the fire. His forehead was furrowed; his disappointment tremendous. Delaney knew he took full responsibility for the situation, as if he could have somehow avoided it. He had lived his life thinking of them, not of himself, and raising them the best he could without a wife. There were few men who could have done as well. Most would have turned a bunch of girls over to an orphanage, a distant relative, or gone out and found a new wife to relieve themselves of the burden. But not Luke McCall. He was as proud of his daughters as if they had been sons. He'd often said he wouldn't trade them for a dozen boys, and he never said anything he didn't mean.

He cleared his throat, having given Delaney's question a moment of serious consideration. "Yes, that's what I've always taught you, and it will always be my basic belief. But we were dealing with Indians or renegades, and in those instances strength *has* come in numbers. This could be different. Hank might be right. I don't want to see us split up any more than you do, Delaney, but it could come to that."

He took a sip of coffee. "I'm sorry, girls. Real sorry that it had to come to this. This isn't the kind of life you deserve, and certainly one I never foresaw as the outcome of our mustanging."

Delaney crossed around the fire and sat next to her father, putting an arm over his shoulder. "Everything will be all right, Daddy. You'll see. By the time we get back to Monterey, Harley will have this mess all cleared up."

None of the girls wanted their father to return to Monterey alone. There was just no telling if there was going to be a bushwhacker out there ready to stop his clock. He wasn't keen on letting any of them go with him and argued until Hank finally used her persuasive talents and convinced him to let her ride along, since she felt responsible for the whole fouled-up affair. He agreed, but only under the condition that she dress up in manly attire to conceal her gender completely and not draw the attention of every gunman out there. That left Andy trying to keep Delaney and Brett from squabbling themselves right into the grave for the next four days while they waited for their father and Hank to return.

She started off by pitting them against each other in a poker game. She even let them take turns winning to keep them happy. The card games helped while away the hours and keep their minds off what might be happening to Hank and their father.

They were about even on their stack of pebbles—which they'd been using as dollar chips—by the time the sun set. They put aside the cards long enough to build a fire and put a pot of coffee on to boil when the soft fall of a horse's hooves sent them reaching for their six-shooters, grabbing their rifles, and taking cover in the trees.

Delaney's heart took off on a high gallop. Hank and

Daddy wouldn't be back for four days . . . unless someone had ambushed them and they were coming back wounded. She feared the horse coming closer might be Daddy's gray or Hank's black, carrying an empty saddle.

"If it's one of Stark's stinking bounty hunters, I'll lay him low," she whispered.

"You'll have to beat me to it," Brett countered.

"Frankly, I don't want to have to kill *any*body," Andy said. "Daddy's right. It's one thing to talk about killing, but when it comes right down to doing it, it's another matter entirely."

The rider came into view, walking his blood bay gelding slowly down the center of the narrow meadow that led to their camp. It wasn't an easy place to stumble onto, which made his presence all the more suspicious.

He halted his horse a hundred feet from the tents. Dusk was descending rapidly, blending everything into shades of gray that blurred clarity. The man wore dark clothes and a black hat. If they hadn't heard him, they might not have even seen him until he was on them. He squinted into the shadows, searching out the camp's occupants.

"Is there anybody here?" He barely elevated his voice, but in the utter stillness and oppressive twilight, the words came loud and clear to the girls' ears.

They huddled together and made no response. They were unsure whether to trust the stranger by giving away their position. Once upon a time they would have welcomed a visitor into their camp, but the whole world had taken on a different tilt now that they had become prey.

The stranger sat his horse like a man who spent more time in the saddle than out, but Delaney detected a wariness in his posture of a man who was accustomed to riding alone and keeping one eye over his shoulder and a hand on his gun.

"Looks like a sundowner," she whispered.

"He's got that lean, hungry look," Brett agreed.

"Okay, so what do we do?" Andy injected.

The rider had advanced to the fire and stepped down from his horse.

Brett's hand shifted on the butt of her Colt. "Makin' himself right at home, isn't he?"

"He probably knows we're here," Andy said. "The way he rode into camp all quiet like, he could have even been watching us for who knows how long."

Brett never took her eyes off the man. "Then if he wanted us dead, we'd already be dead instead of sitting here acting like a bunch of scared jackrabbits hiding in the bushes."

"Well, all the circulation is gone out of my legs from the knees down," Delaney stated. "So if we're gonna make a move, I'd say it had better be pretty quick."

"You're elected," Andy said.

Actually, Delaney didn't mind. She knew she was the best for the job, except for maybe Brett. They were cut from the same cloth; everybody said that was why they didn't get along worth a tinker's damn. They all four had their qualities—or faults, if you will—and Delaney's was being inflexible. She could stare down a rattler and bluff a bear back into his cave. She could look right mean when she had a mind to.

The stranger lowered himself to his haunches and was about to reach for one of the tin coffee cups when Delaney's voice, cold and hard and low, stopped him dead in his tracks.

"That's about far enough, mister. If you don't want a bullet messin' up that pretty face of yours, you'd be wise to toss your iron over there in the weeds, including all your spares. And don't try anything. I'd just as soon shoot you as look at you."

The stranger came back to his full height in slow motion, his hands a good distance from his sidearm. "Don't shoot.

I'm throwing my gun down now." Using only his fingertips, he pulled the six-shooter out of its holster and carefully set it down on Andy's blankets four feet away as if it meant as much to him as a newborn baby to its mama.

"All right," Delaney responded. "Now the spares in your boots and behind your back. And that Bowie on your hip."

The stranger, still moving cautiously, produced a knife from his right boot and placed it next to the Colt.

"Come on, mister. I want your hideout gun."

"I don't use one. Don't need to."

"We'll see about that." Delaney whispered to her sisters to stay put for the time being. "No sense in him knowing what cards are in the hole." She eased from her squat and stood a second to get the blood flowing back into her legs. Warily she moved toward the stranger, her Henry rifle aimed at his midsection.

The man's eyes lit with surprise. "Why, you're a woman."

Delaney didn't like the look that crossed his face. Didn't like the way he suddenly relaxed his guard as if she were no threat. "A trigger isn't a hard thing to pull, mister, even for a woman. So don't get too comfortable with your situation. There's enough gunpowder here to make you look like a tin can hit with buckshot. Are you alone?"

He pulled up his guard again; his gaze slid over her and searched out the advancing darkness behind her. But he couldn't see the others. The twins would stay out of sight and keep him wondering just where they were and how many they were in number. "I asked you a question, mister, and I don't recall getting an answer."

"I'm alone. You can tell the others to come out. That is, if you're not bluffing."

"I never bluff. Now, move over there by that tree and put your arms around it," Delaney commanded. "Hug it real good like it was your sweetheart."

"All I wanted was some company and a cup of coffee, ma'am."

"We'll commence a discussion as soon as I decide whether or not you're here with dishonorable intentions."

He shook his head as if exasperated. "I'm beginning to think I should have ridden the other way. You wanted by the law or something?"

"Where are you from, mister? Back East?"

"Texas."

"Humph. I might have known. Only a greenhorn or a Texan would ask somebody a question like that. Now, the tree."

His gaze held hers for a moment as each tried to read the other, then he shrugged and obeyed her order. She waited until he had his arms around it as far as they would go and his face was pressed sufficiently against the bark, then she motioned for Brett and Andy to join her. He turned his head as he heard them approach. He didn't say anything, but Delaney didn't miss his half-grin as he saw they were women too.

"What's this? A ladies' circle camp fire meeting?"

Delaney pressed the Henry into his lower back. "You won't think it's so amusing when you find yourself trying to convince St. Peter to let you through the Golden Gate."

Brett and Andy held their guns on him while Delaney felt around his back and legs for a hideout gun, or another knife. She found nothing. She still didn't trust him, but she finally stepped back a fair distance.

All three of them eased back to the fire. "All right," Delaney commanded. "We'll have that little tête-a-tête now, starting with why you're out here."

He stood by the tree for another minute or so, then

glanced at the coffee pot with a hungry look in his eyes. "Mind if we discuss it over a cup of that fine-smelling coffee?"

"I suppose we can."

"Help yourself to those soda biscuits too," Andy offered, acting like he was Sunday company. Then, at Delaney's flash of disgust at her generosity, she added, "They aren't much good when they get cold."

"Much obliged, ma'am. Maybe it'll take away the jitters."

He took after the biscuits like he hadn't eaten for at least two days. They watched him like hawks surveying a corn field. When he had downed a half cup of coffee, he said, "It tastes as good as it smells. That's how I found you. The aroma just seemed to drift out into the hills."

"You kin to a bloodhound?"

The stranger smiled and locked horns with Delaney again. Something tripped inside her, something quite unlike anything she'd ever felt before when she'd looked at a man. She suddenly felt like maybe a strong cup of coffee would take away some of her own jitters too.

She set about pouring it, and one for the twins, while they continued to hold their guns on the stranger.

"So what brought you over here," Brett picked up the interrogation. "Aside from the coffee, that is."

He was free enough with the information. "Actually, I was workin' on a ranch down near Los Angeles. I got tired of the heat and the scenery and speaking Spanish, so I figured I'd just ride for a spell. See where the wind blows me. I heard about the stampede to the new diggings at Meadow Lake."

"You missed the stampede," Andy informed him. "It ended a year ago."

He shrugged indifferently. "There's always disillusioned miners ready to sell their claims. Besides, the men who make it rich aren't the ones panning and digging, but the ones selling supplies and cattle and horses to the rest of them."

"Or the ones waylaying the gold shipments," Delaney remarked cryptically.

He lifted his eyes to Delaney's. A half-curious smile played on his lips. "Don't tell me you three are a band of outlaws?"

"We thought you might be in that line of work yourself," she replied coolly.

"I'm a jack of all trades, ma'am, but stealing from innocent, hard-working people isn't one of them. So, what brings you gals out here all alone?"

"Horses," Andy lied as smoothly as she dealt Blackjack. "We've got us a ranch not far from here. A wild stallion took off with a bunch of our brood mares. We're trying to get them back."

"Oh. I was sort of hoping you might be heading north. I wouldn't mind having some company."

"Sorry, mister."

He accepted the mild rebuff and sipped at his coffee, seemingly as content as a tick in a dog's ear. Delaney wondered if he figured to just make himself at home. He must have read her mind, or at least the disapproving glare in her eyes, because he finally drained the cup and rose to his feet.

"Well, ladies, I'd better be on my way. I do appreciate your hospitality. Would you know of a good place to camp around here?"

"If you go up the creek a mile or two, you'll find a likely spot," Brett subtly urged. Normally they wouldn't have been so unfriendly, but the circumstances certainly changed the complexion of things.

He nodded, not fooled by their anxiousness to have him gone, and the farther away, the better. "I'll need my weapons back," he gently reminded them with his most winning smile.

Apprehensively, Delaney rose and collected the hardware. Brett and Andy guarded him until he'd re-armed himself and swung into the saddle. "It's been a pleasure, ladies." He touched the brim of his hat in farewell. "Until we meet again."

Delaney had mixed feelings about whether she wanted that to happen, but there was one thing she was certain of: she had detected the scent of tobacco on him. The same scent left by the intruder in the *cabaña*.

Sam Saxton stretched out next to his campfire and pulled the photograph out of his shirt. By firelight, he stared at it, thinking that those McCall women were among the prettiest he'd ever seen. Seeing them in person, even in men's clothing, hadn't changed his opinion. If anything, their unbound curves had ignited a disturbing desire that wedged its way between what he was being paid to do and what he wanted to do. Admittedly, the fact that he was dragging his heels probably had something to do with that.

He traced a finger over the face of the black-haired one, the one who'd sauntered up to him with a rifle pointed at his private parts as if she wouldn't have any qualms at all about turning him into a gelding. He didn't understand the notion that had slipped into his head at the sight of her, but at least she wasn't the one he had agreed to take back to Stark. The one that had fit Henrietta McCall's description, as given to him by Stark, and by the photograph, had not been present.

One way or the other, he figured he'd be able to walk right into their camp when the other two returned. Now that they thought they knew him, he doubted any of them would lift an eyebrow. This whole thing had been easy, much too easy, but he didn't feel guilty about upping the ante. Men like Stark needed to pay, one way or the other.

CHAPTER EIGHT

QUITTIN' THE FLAT

Delaney and the twins saw no more sign of the dark-haired stranger and figured they'd sufficiently scared him off. They were glad he must have been exactly who he said he was. Otherwise, he'd have had them in cuffs and escorting them back to the gallows by now.

Delaney, for one, had lost a whole night's sleep thinking about him. It irritated her, but she supposed it was understandable because, as Andy put it, that man had been about as pretty as a Royal Flush.

They were mostly surprised to see their father and Hank ride into camp a whole day early on lathered horses. It brought them to attention, knowing inherently that something was wrong.

Luke McCall swung out of the saddle while Old Dan was skidding to a halt. "Let's get this camp moved," he ordered without so much as a howdy-do. "Harley's dead and Stark's blaming it on us." He removed the folded newspaper from his saddlebags and handed it to Delaney and the twins. "We made the front page. The accusation has Monterey in an uproar. At least the people who know us. And there's considerable backlash by the publisher, our good friend Crosby Bennett."

Delaney and the twins were still confused, unable to absorb it all at once.

"We got jumped by another bounty hunter," Luke continued. "Hank got him, though, so he won't be bothering us again."

They turned to Hank. She had alighted from her black but was just standing there, looking dazed.

"You killed another man?" Delaney asked, dismayed.

"She had no choice." Luke spoke up for her. "If she hadn't, I'd be dead. She would be too. Now, come on. Let's get out of here. There's no tellin' how many more are after us. Those Wanted posters must be circulating pretty good by now. This newspaper story will make matters worse."

"What happened to Harley? Didn't he get a chance to talk to Stark?"

Luke threw the packsaddle on one of the spare horses and started cinching it down. "Harley was found dead, bushwhacked a few miles out of Hawk's Point. I suspect he spoke to Stark on our behalf and then Stark killed him on his way back to Monterey."

Delaney felt like she'd been punched in the gut. She had liked Harley. They all had. She lowered herself to a rock and put her head between her hands. "How are we ever going to get out of this mess, Daddy?"

"Kill Stark," Brett stated in a voice as bitter as twice-boiled coffee.

"That might eliminate the driving force behind this," Luke conceded, "but Stark's set something even bigger into motion that won't stop until we're all dead."

"But we're innocent!" Andy blurted angrily. It was her turn to pace the camp, fired up by the injustice of it all.

Luke finished cinching the saddle and started collecting their belongings. "I figure the best thing to do is get you girls out of harm's way. They'll figure we'll head south to Mexico, so we're going north. We'll go into Nevada, to Virginia City.

I'll get you girls set up over there and then I'll come back and try to find a way to get this straightened out. Maybe I can get someone to act as a liaison with the U.S. Marshal or the governor."

Delaney rose to her feet again. "We won't leave you, Daddy."

He took her shoulders gently in his big hands. "This is one time you have no choice, Delaney. The bounty hunters will be looking for the five of us. I'll have a better chance of getting things turned around if I'm alone. And I want you girls in a safe place."

Hank still looked dazed. "We're leaving a trail of dead bodies. Pretty soon nobody is going to believe that it's all been in self-defense. We already know if bounty hunters find us, we're as good as dead. We'll never even make it to trial."

"All we can do is take this one step at a time," Luke tried to assure them. "The first step is to clear this up without any more bloodshed."

Delaney began stashing her belongings in her saddlebags. "Bloodshed or not, I can only say one thing—Eli Stark had better stay out of my gun sights. I've had my fill of that double-dealing mongrel."

A shadow rider is someone who thinks he looks so fine atop a horse that he rides with one eye on his own shadow. Delaney was watching her shadow and that of the others, not because she was impressed by their posture in the saddle, but because she could look at the shadows and momentarily detach herself from reality. She could imagine they were just heading through the Salinas Mountains to chase more mustangs, not running for their lives.

The shadows, shifting and changing, shrinking and expanding against the hills that ran alongside them, enabled her to separate herself from the fear, and from the realization that their lives might be merging into a future that would forevermore hold no resemblance to the past, a future that could end any second with a bullet.

They'd never had to watch their back trail or mind the hoofprints they'd left behind. They'd never had to search the hills with their field glasses for anything except wild horses and renegades. For the most part, even outlaws stuck to the settlements where life was easy and crimes were accessible. In all their years of mustanging, they'd never run into anybody who wanted to hurt them.

Being hunted brought a different mind-set, and Delaney felt as if she had to go faster and faster to put time and distance between them and the predators who would stay relentlessly on their trail until they got their bounty.

The five of them avoided the skyline and took the trails they had used dozens of times before. Dusk stole their shadows and darkness draped them in its protective cloak as they rode down into the Salinas River Valley and hit the stage road. They paced their horses and rode on into the night when travelers were not so likely to see them. There was no time for disguises and subterfuge. Their purpose was speed. Their destination the Great Valley, away from the coastal towns where they were known, and where Eli Stark and his bounty hunters would be lying in wait.

For the first few days, they rested their horses in the daylight and in the cover of trees. By a half moon and starlit sky they hurried through the many valleys of the Gabilans and dropped down to the San Benito River. From there they rode toward Panoche Pass in the Diablo Range.

They slept very little and suffered the heat and dust, and the scant meals and aching bodies in silence. It never occurred to any of them to complain. As Luke McCall had always said, "Kicking never gets you anywhere, unless you're a mule."

They gave themselves and their horses another solid rest before heading into the pass at daybreak. They took the steep descent slowly and carefully—they didn't need a horse going lame—but once in the Great Valley they rode fast and unrestricted. They rode by daylight now because they saw no movement save their own across the yellow and brown hills of early fall. They felt relatively safe that they had eluded anyone who might be after them.

But once, for a fleeting moment atop Jackass Grade, Delaney caught sight of a lone rider behind them, silhouetted against the skyline.

"There." She pointed. "On the ridge. Do you see him?"

The others searched, but the rider dropped out of sight before they could spot him.

"I wonder if it's that guy who was heading to the gold fields," Brett said.

Luke McCall leaned forward in the saddle, putting Old Dan into motion again. "Let's keep moving. Whoever he is, I intend to lose him in Sacramento."

Delaney paced the hotel room in her underwear, going every few minutes to the window to peek out past the shades at the street below. Behind an ornate, hand-painted dressing screen, Hank sat in a tub full of lavender-scented water.

"I don't like it," Delaney lamented. "Daddy's been gone a long time."

"It takes a while to check things out without drawing attention to yourself," Hank replied from behind the screen. "Why don't you sit down and play me a song on your harmonica. You're moving those feet like a scared centipede."

Delaney attempted a song but her heart wasn't in it. She

gave up and returned to the window to watch the busy street and the sea of unfamiliar faces. "What if someone recognizes him? That guy I saw following us might not have been the one who came to camp at all, but some stinking bounty hunter. If those Wanted posters have gotten this far . . . well, I just don't have a good feeling."

"I'd like to enjoy this bath, Delaney. Don't get me all in a knot. I just hate it when you get your premonitions. There's too many times they come true."

Delaney knew she shouldn't get herself worked up either. Their father had just gone to check on the horses and take a look around to see if the Wanted poster was tacked on the wall at the sheriff's office. She always got nervous when one of the family was separated from the rest and didn't return when she figured they should. She knew she worried unduly, but she couldn't seem to change that aspect of her personality.

"Nobody's going to recognize me from that poster anyway," he'd assured them, "and especially if I'm alone. You girls get cleaned up and get your bellies full, then we'll head out."

From behind the divider, Hank said, "We'll get this straightened out, and we'll be back to mustanging before you know it."

Delaney lifted the shade more to get a better view of the street. "How can you not be afraid? We've killed two men."

"*I've* killed two men."

"I was right by your side on the first one, and they were both done to protect Daddy. I would have done the same thing. Besides, we stick together. The McCalls always stick together."

It was a moment before Hank responded. "I'm scared silly, Delaney. I might have had just cause to do it, but it doesn't make it any easier to live with. I keep seeing it, even in my dreams. I could hang for it, too, if a judge and jury don't happen to see it in the same light. We're outlaws now, thanks to those Wanted posters and the newspapers picking up the story. Why, there will probably be writers looking for fast money who'll sensationalize the story and turn us into 'bandit queens,' or something equally ridiculous."

"Well, I feel like a broomtail in a box canyon," Delaney replied. "I'm either going to have to fly or die. Oh, no—"

"What?" Hank demanded, alarmed by the change in Delaney's tone.

"That guy that came to our camp is across the street."

"What's he doing?"

"Just standing there, leaning against the saloon, smoking a cigarette."

Hank came out from behind the screen, wrapping herself in a towel. Together they peered around the edge of the shade.

"Which one is he?"

"There, in front of the Gold Bar Saloon. The tall one with the broad shoulders, dark clothing."

"Oh, he *is* good looking."

"Pretty as a stallion running wild."

Hank gave Delaney a curious look. "What's this? Professed single woman of the McCall family notices a man?"

Delaney scowled. "Oh, hush. It's nothing. I can appreciate good horse flesh when I see it. It doesn't mean I'm going to run out and buy it. I find it suspicious anyway that he's right across the street from our hotel. It's almost like he's following us."

"Maybe he's staying here too. If he was after us, he could have had you and the twins easily enough back at camp. Then he could have just laid in wait for me and Daddy to ride in."

Almost as if the stranger had sensed he was being watched, he left his post and sauntered down the boardwalk, crossed the street and disappeared up an alley. Hank went back behind the screen to finish drying off and dressing.

Shortly, maid service arrived to carry away Hank's bath water and bring fresh bucketfuls for Delaney. She was up to her neck in lavender-scented bubbles when a knock sounded at the door and an envelope appeared on the carpet from underneath.

Hank hurried to collect it, but when she opened the door to see who had left it, no one was there. She looked up and down the hall and saw only a man's boot heel disappearing around the corner.

"That's odd," Hank said.

"Who is it?"

Hank closed the door. "Nobody. Just a note."

"Well, what does it say?"

Hank stood near the screen and opened the envelope. Delaney heard her gasp.

"Hank, what *is* it?"

"My God, Delaney. Stark's in town."

CHAPTER NINE

CLAWING LEATHER

Delaney shot out of the tub quicker than hell can scorch a feather. She grabbed a towel, brushed off the water, and yanked on riding clothes over her half-wet skin. Hank tore out to warn her father and the twins. She was moving so fast, Delaney could almost see the dust flying from her heels.

Later, Delaney was glad she took that bath. It turned out to be a good long while before she saw lavender soap again.

Hank burst back into the room a few minutes later, breathing like a winded horse. "I met Daddy in the hall. He saw Stark and Stark saw him."

Delaney hopped around on one foot trying to get her boots on. "Was it him behind us the whole time?"

Hank shook her head. "I don't know, but we've got to get out of here."

Hank packed their belongings. Delaney finally got her boots on and pitched in. When they had everything crammed into their packs, they headed out the door and met the others in the hall. They slowed their pace to the livery to keep from drawing undue attention.

Delaney reached the open livery doors first, but she stopped so abruptly that the others plowed into her.

"What in tarnation—"

A young, wide-eyed stable boy was standing there holding

the reins of their five horses and two pack horses. They were all saddled, bridled and ready to go.

"Some feller ran in here just a smokin' and threw on the saddles for you," the words spilled from the boy's mouth. "Said you'd be in a hurry. Paid your bill too. Here"—he thrust the reins at them—"you'd best be shakin' a leg."

Dumbfounded, the McCalls tied their gear down, grabbed leather, and swung into their saddles.

"Who was he?" Luke asked as Old Dan excitedly circled the buckskin.

"Don't know. Didn't give his name. He's wasn't the sort you want to question."

"I hope this isn't a set-up by Stark," Hank said.

"Well, let's not sit here jawing about it." Brett put her heels to her sorrel and headed into sunlight.

They hit the street on a lope, weaving through wagons and pedestrians. A shout went up behind them. They turned simultaneously in their saddles and saw Stark running down the street after them, gun drawn.

"Stop! Stop those riders! It's the McCall gang!"

Brett saw an opening and kicked her horse into a gallop, clearing a path for the others. Shots rang out. The McCalls leaned low over their horses' necks and made for the open road. It wasn't until they reined up five miles later that Delaney saw the blood on their daddy's shirt.

Eli Stark tried to get off another shot but knew it would be a wasted bullet. The McCalls were too far away. He vented his spleen of every profanity he knew and headed for the livery boy who had taken cover behind some sacks of oats.

"You, boy! Get my—"

Something cold and hard pressed into the side of his neck. "Disregard that order, young man. This man won't be going anywhere but back to Hawk's Point."

Eli slowly swiveled his head and found himself staring into the deadly eyes of Sam Saxton. "What do you think you're doing?"

The bounty hunter ran the muzzle of the six-shooter up Eli's neck to the base of his ear. "You know, boss, I'm getting mighty tired of reminding you that you're paying *me* to bring in those outlaws without interference from you or anybody else."

Eli refused to show fear. "And I see you're doing a fine job of it, Saxton."

"What are you doing here, Stark?" The gun made a deeper impression in Eli's neck.

"I followed you. I figured I might be of some use."

"I work alone. All you've accomplished is putting them on the run again."

"Why should you care as long as you get your money? Don't tell me you're a bounty hunter with morals?"

"I care about one thing, Stark: our deal. And you keep breaking the rules. There are too many gold towns up and down these mountains to count, and the McCalls could be headed for any one of them."

"You're supposed to be the best tracker around. Came highly recommended."

"In case you hadn't noticed, they headed right down the stage road. How long do you think it'll be before their tracks are obliterated by a thousand others?"

"They won't be going far. I hit McCall."

Eli saw Saxton's eyes flare. Was it surprise, or anger? Or both?

"That'll slow 'em down," Stark added. "They'll be searchin' for a doctor."

Saxton holstered his sidearm. "You're on your own, Stark.

See if you can pick up their trail by yourself."

Saxton started to walk away. With him went Eli's ace in the hole. He knew he couldn't find the McCalls on his own. All he could do was try to keep Saxton in sight. Panic consumed him; he broke out in a cold sweat.

"Don't be so hasty, Saxton. I'm just anxious not to let those killers get away."

Saxton was unsympathetic. "Justice isn't at the bottom of this, Stark. Lust is. And from what I've heard about your dealings, I wouldn't be a bit surprised to find out you've framed the McCalls."

"I'll give you an extra five hundred dollars. Just don't quit. I can't keep searching anyway. I've left a deputy in charge at Hawk's Point and I need to head back. I was just hoping to wrap this up quickly."

"It won't happen now, thanks to your interference."

"All right," Eli tried for contriteness. "I'll back out. What do you say?"

"To the five hundred?"

"That's right."

For a second, when Saxton looked up the road in the direction the McCalls had gone, Eli thought he saw something flicker in his eyes.

"You've got a deal, Stark. But I'll kill you if you butt in again. *Or* if you send more of your boys to undercut me."

"I understand. Now, you'd best be lighting a shuck. They'll be so far ahead you'll never catch up."

"I'll just follow the trail of blood," Saxton said derisively.

Eli watched Saxton saunter into the livery and casually collect his horse. The two-bit gunslinger acted like he was running the show. Well, regardless of what he'd said, Eli wasn't going to let him out of his sight. He wasn't going to pay him twenty-five hundred dollars either. No, sir. As soon as Saxton located the McCalls again, he'd be finding himself riding a white horse home.

Fear nearly choked off Delaney's words. "My God, Daddy. You've been hit."

Luke McCall's lips thinned to a grim line as he unknotted his bandanna with one hand and pulled it from around his neck. "Caught a bullet. Don't worry, I'll be fine."

Delaney wasn't so sure of that. Her sisters wore expressions just as apprehensive. A trunk wound was never something to take lightly. They wanted to take a closer look at the wound, but he refused. "We haven't got time for that. I'll just wrap it for now."

He looped his reins around the saddle horn and packed the bandanna inside his shirt, trying not to flinch. The girls removed their bandannas too. Hank took them, square-knotted them together, then sidled her bay up alongside Old Dan. With Delaney's help from the other side, they tied the bandannas around his waist to hold the makeshift bandage in place.

"It's not bleeding too much," Luke tried to assure them. "I think it just grazed me. Nothing serious."

"We need to get you to a doctor," Andy said.

Luke glanced nervously over his shoulder. "Stark'll be on our trail. We can't tarry."

"Let's keep to the stage road," Hank suggested. "They can't pick out our tracks as easily."

"Won't he figure out we've gone straight over the mountains into Nevada?" Delaney kept an eye on the road behind them, wondering how long it would take Stark to saddle up, maybe even gather a posse.

"We'll leave the road at Auburn, make it look like we're headed south," Luke said.

Brett held her reins high as her nervous sorrel paced in circles around the others. "But we don't know the country past Sacramento."

"I was in this country back in '49 and '50," Luke replied, looking frightfully pale. "After we get to Emigrant Gap, there's only one way over the Sierras."

"Then let's get going."

They hurried back onto the stage road, riding in two groups to reduce drawing attention to themselves. A cold lump settled in Delaney's gut as they paced their horses over the next few miles. She wouldn't voice her growing fear, but she prayed their father could make the grueling ride over the Sierras. It was also late enough in the season that the weather could change suddenly in the high country. It was no place for an injured man.

They rode the last five miles to Auburn in the dark and found a secluded camping spot in some heavy growth a mile from town. The girls laid out their father's blankets and brought him water and hardtack. He was interested only in the water. They fussed over him, each contributing something from her saddlebags to use as bandage material. The bleeding had slowed, but there was no telling what damage the slug had done to his insides. He insisted it wasn't deep, just under the skin, that he could even feel it. But his confident attitude didn't calm the girls' fears.

"We need to get you to a doctor," Andy reiterated. "Please let us take you into Auburn."

"Stark probably knows he hit me. A doctor's office is the first place he'll look." Luke shook his head glumly. "No, the best way not to be followed is not to leave any tracks at all."

Andy persisted. "Even if he does, we can get you treated and be gone."

Luke held his ground. "We've got to lose ourselves in these hills so he'd have to search every mining town in the Sierras to find us. Besides, I'll bet a doctor would just leave the bullet in there. For the most part, they don't like to go digging."

At their dubious expressions, he added, "I won't be the first man packing a bullet. The body heals up around some of them. Why, sometimes those old bullets even work themselves out, given time."

The girls knew what he said was true, but they also knew that if the bullet had gone into his intestines, or had carried with it bits of cloth or dirt, it could produce poisons that would spread throughout his body and kill him. Or he could bleed to death internally. They also knew that probing for it could cause the same result. It didn't make it any easier to sit by and do nothing. In the end, they didn't argue with him.

While they dipped hardtack into their coffee, he drifted off to sleep. They spoke in low tones to keep from waking him.

"This makes me furious enough to gun Stark down on sight," Brett whispered angrily. "There's no call for this. None of it. And if Daddy dies—"

Hank sat across the fire from Brett, her forearms resting on her knees. She hung her head. "I should have married Stark. It's all because of me."

Andy immediately put her arm across Hank's shoulders. "You can't take the blame for this, Hank. None of us was willing to sacrifice you to save our own necks. Least of all Daddy."

Hank drew in a deep breath then released it slowly. "Maybe not, but how will I ever live with myself if he dies, knowing I could have prevented all this. I could still go to Stark. Surrender. Make a deal. He just wants me humbled.

He'd probably be willing to drop his vendetta if he thinks he's won."

Delaney paced around the fire. "That's not the answer. It won't take back the bullet in Daddy's stomach. The answer is killing that sonofabitch."

"We'd just be in deeper than we are now," Hank replied dismally.

"Maybe, but at least there would be a legitimate reason for hanging us."

Hank's temper flared and she leaped to her feet. "You don't understand, do you? This isn't a game. I could stop this. I could stop this right now!" She stalked off into the darkness to be alone.

Delaney settled next to Brett. "With the mood she's in, sis, we'd better keep an eye on her. I wouldn't put it past her to do something stupid."

Auburn squatted like a dozing beast in the coming darkness. One eye opened and a light appeared, then another. By the time Eli Stark had reached the town's perimeter, the beast was wide awake and staring at him with a thousand eyes.

He made a bee-line to the doctor's office and found that no one had been there matching Luke McCall's description.

Stark then went to all four liveries in town. He didn't think the McCalls would be so stupid as to stay in town now that they knew he was close, but he figured maybe the livery boys had seen them, or Saxton.

The last hostler lifted his muscled shoulders. "I got all these horses to take care of, mister, and I ain't got time to stand in the doorway and watch the comings and goings of this town. Auburn's a crossroads. We get lots of traffic from the gold fields."

A blond-haired boy about eight years old ran out from the

back of the barn and overhead their conversation. "I saw a man come riding through town on a horse that looked like the one you described," he offered eagerly. "A pretty bay gelding."

Stark moved closer to the boy. "Which direction did he go?"

"I was up in the loft when I saw him, so I had a good view as he rode out of town. Looked to me like he was taking the road to Grass Valley."

Stark dug in his vest pocket and found two-bits. He tossed it to the kid. Then he left his horse and headed to a hotel. He would get a good night's rest. It shouldn't be too hard to get Saxton within sight tomorrow.

A hand on her shoulder brought Delaney awake with a start, reaching for the .44 at her side. She heard her father say, "We need to get moving."

The half moon was resting low on the western horizon, and the first gray dawning was showing in the east. It all came flooding back then, and Delaney wanted to bawl.

She sat up and saw that her sisters were already moving about. "Are you all right, Daddy?" She knew it was a stupid question. Of course he wasn't all right. At least he was still alive.

He'd wiped out the fire. The moonlight caught in his eyes and reflected pain—and the hot, glassy veil of fever. He said, "I'll be all right."

They saddled up and Luke McCall led the way from the trees, easing Old Dan quietly through the underbrush and over the rocks. The gelding seemed to know that stealth and caution were expected of him. The girls stayed in the deep shadows waiting for Luke's signal to proceed. Then, single-file, they emerged onto the stage road and headed straight for Colfax.

There was no traffic on the road in the pre-dawn, but movement picked up shortly after daybreak. They split up into groups again even though no one seemed interested in them. By late afternoon, they sat astride their tired horses on a hill overlooking Dutch Flat. Up ahead loomed the Sierras, and on the other side of town they saw a bunch of emigrants who had just traveled over the mountains from the east.

"If we circled the town and came in from the other side," Hank said, "then everybody would assume we came in with the emigrants."

Delaney took the opportunity to study her father while his attention was elsewhere. His reflexes had slowed. The fever in his eyes had deepened. "If we did that, we could probably get Daddy to a doctor."

Luke shook his head stubbornly. "It's too risky to be seen in town. If Stark tracks us this far and talks to anybody who's seen us, he'll know for sure we're headed to Nevada. I've got to get you girls to safety. Now, let's go. I want to set up camp on the other side of Dutch Flat before dark."

"Daddy, you're going to die if you don't consent to see a doctor," Brett admonished.

For possibly the first time in her life, Delaney was going to disobey her father's wishes. "Stark will be a year of Sundays checking out every town in the gold fields to see where we went," she said. "We've stayed on the main road the whole time, except to camp, and even then we were careful not to leave tracks. I don't see how he could know for sure which way we went. Besides, if we're going to head up into the mountains, we're going to need some supplies and warm coats, even if you refuse to see a doctor."

The fever had clearly dulled Luke McCall's thinking, but

the one thought he clung to was that he needed to get them to safety. He repeated it again.

"If you die," Andy argued, gently but firmly, "then we really will be on our own. Think about that, Daddy."

He did, but in the end it did nothing to change his mind about seeing a doctor. He did agree to Hank's suggestion, though. "We'll circle around to the other side of town. While you girls are setting up camp, I'll take one of you and go get what we'll need at the general store. But stay clear of the emigrants. We don't want people to get close enough to find out you're women."

"I'll go with you," Delaney volunteered. "I can pass for a boy quicker than the others can as long as there isn't any long hair hanging from under my hat."

With apprehension darkening his visage, Luke nudged Old Dan and started the wide loop to the other side of town. A mile out, they left Hank and the twins then circled back. At the emigrant camp they drew curious glances, but outside of a few "howdy-do's," they spoke to no one.

Delaney kept her head tilted so that her hat brim shadowed all of her face from the nose up. To the emigrants they probably appeared to be just a tired father and his son on their way to good fortune in golden California.

They took the center of main street, observing the town's prosperity and permanency. There were dozens of businesses, including three schools, an opera house, a Methodist Church, the Dutch Flat Hotel, Masonic Halls, and the stage depot.

They spotted a couple of general stores and stopped at the first one. Delaney swung from the saddle and noticed her father slumped forward, holding onto the saddle horn. He was barely able to get his leg over the high-backed saddle. Once his feet were on the ground, he paused, slump-shouldered, collecting himself. He'd been two days without eating, and the wound had not looked good this morning when they'd changed the dressing.

Delaney slid under her horse's neck and took his arm. "Daddy, you look terrible."

He managed a weak smile. "I'll be fine."

She didn't believe one word of it. It took every ounce of his strength just to loop the reins over the hitching rail and walk into the general store. He certainly wouldn't make it over the Sierras.

Inside, he made his way to the counter to give the store-keeper his list of supplies. He tried to hide his wound by keeping his arm bent across his mid-section. Delaney slid from view in the ready-made clothing section and searched for warm coats and hats and gloves. The store was well-stocked, probably due to the amount of emigrant traffic they received, but she only selected two coats and two sets of gloves. They didn't want curiosities raised about buying five of everything—just in case Stark came in asking questions—so they planned to get the other coats and gloves in other stores around town.

Delaney was just stepping out from behind the coat rack when she heard the proprietor release a startled expletive. She bolted forward. But she wasn't quick enough to break her father's fall to the hardwood floor.

CHAPTER TEN

EMPTY SADDLE

The storekeeper knelt next to Luke and eyed the bloody bandage. "This man is hurt," he said, giving Delaney an accusatory look. "Shouldn't he be seeing a doctor?"

Delaney dropped down on the other side of her father. When she saw that he wasn't dead, she breathed a sigh of relief. Affecting a male-sounding voice, she said, "I've been trying to get him to one, mister, but he has no use for doctors."

"I'd say he's no longer in a position to be choosy."

With no ifs, ands, or buts, the storekeeper pulled Luke up onto his burly shoulder and headed for the back door, leaving Delaney no choice but to follow.

"Where are you going with my father?" she demanded. "You can't just do that."

"I'm taking him to Miss Laura's right next door. She's a doctor. And a fine one at that."

Delaney was frightened half out of her wits and didn't know what to do. Her father wasn't going to be happy to have people know he'd been shot. They'd want to know how it happened. They might call in the town marshal. What if those Wanted posters had reached these parts by now? Stark would have made sure all the doctors got one.

She heeled the storekeeper across the narrow alley and into the back door of the doctor's office. A small shingle next to the door read: L. J. Hogan, M.D.

The lady doctor was red-headed and pretty, and she sat at a big oak desk reading some sort of encyclopedia or medical book. She jumped right up when she saw them and rushed forward to lend assistance.

"Just stretch him out there on the table, Doyle."

Dr. L. J. Hogan immediately set to work moving Luke's vest and shirt out of the way and shooting questions fast and furious at Delaney who did the only thing she could do. She lied.

"It was my fault," she said. "I was aiming at a pine hen in the mountains and Daddy just happened to step out of the trees right in front of the bullet. It happened a couple days ago, but Daddy says it just grazed him and he saw no need to go to a doctor."

The doctor seemed to know she was lying, but she didn't press for the truth. She focused on the wound, removing their makeshift bandage and surveying the damage. "If there was major internal damage or bleeding, he probably wouldn't be alive. At least that's encouraging, but he has abdominal pain which means there could be bowel damage. I'll need to go in and take a look to be certain."

The storekeeper sidled his way to the back door. "If you won't be needing me, Miss Laura, I'd better get back to my store."

Dr. Hogan was all business; she didn't look up. "I'll holler if I need you to handle the chloroform."

The doctor gently cleaned around the wound. "Doyle always offers to help." She spoke as she worked. "But the poor man passes out if things get too messy." She gave Delaney a measured look. "You don't look weak-kneed, young lady. How about you helping me. Take off your hat, roll up your sleeves, and I'll have *you* handle the chloroform."

It upset Delaney to think the doctor had seen right through her disguise, but all she said was, "If you're talking about cuttin' on him, then I think he'd better be the one to decide whether he's going to let you do that."

"You don't think he'd trust a woman doctor?" A perfectly arched brow lifted as she eyed Delaney with almost a hint of amusement.

"He wouldn't give one hoot what you've got under your skirt. All he cares about is if you've got a brain in your head. He knows women are as capable as men."

That answer pleased her. "There are plenty of people who wouldn't agree."

Delaney shrugged. "I've never let being female stop me from doing anything."

Dr. Hogan ran a glance over her attire. "No, I can see you haven't."

Luke McCall stirred. In another second his eyes opened, confused and feverish.

"You passed out in the store, Daddy," Delaney was quick to explain before he said something he shouldn't. "There happened to be a doctor right next door and the storekeeper insisted on hauling you over here. The doctor here wants to go after that bullet in your belly. I told her she'd have to ask you for permission."

Luke's head had cleared some and he turned it so he could see the red-headed woman standing by his side. He figured her to be in her late forties. She was real pretty, but he supposed it was the candid look in her large green eyes and the confident set to her mouth that made him relax. It didn't change anything though.

"I don't have time to be cut up. I need to be in Sacramento in a couple of days. A business deal," he lied. "I can't be laid up here or I'll miss the opportunity of a lifetime."

"Well, sir," Dr. Hogan said bluntly, "the way things look right now, it had *better* be the deal of a lifetime because you can probably count your remaining days on one hand."

Luke and Delaney exchanged frightened glances.

Dr. Hogan continued, "If the bullet hasn't torn you up too much inside, I might be able to save you."

"How are you going to determine that?"

"I'll make an incision."

"Cut me open?"

"There is a tremendous risk in operative intervention," she admitted. "Most physicians choose inactive treatment for this kind of wound. But, as I said, there is about the same degree of risk in leaving the bullet in there as there is attempting to remove it. Wound infection is the main culprit, but antiseptic wound care is coming much in vogue now, with wonderful results. You can be assured that I keep up to date on all medical advances.

"Personally, I am of the philosophy that a physician has to be able to get to the problem to fix it. However, if the bullet miraculously missed your intestines and other vital organs, then you might survive without intervention. I've seen men recover from gut wounds without surgery, but I can tell you that most don't. And death can be long and painful. The alternative would be for me to give you opium or morphine to quiet the bowel and leave the bullet in there. If you survive, it'll mean the bullet miraculously missed all major organs. If there is significant damage to the intestinal tract, though, then inactive treatment would result in eventual death from peritonitis. At least we can assume there was no significant damage to a blood vessel, or you would have already bled to death.

"If surgery is an option for you, I'll use chloroform to put you under. Your daughter will be here with you at all times, assisting me."

"You're throwing a lot at us at once, Doc," Luke managed. "I think I need a few minutes to think about it."

"That's fine. I'll leave you alone with your daughter to discuss it."

After she was gone from the room, Delaney watched her father close his eyes. Every word the doctor had said was sinking into his feverish mind. When, at last, he looked up at Delaney's waiting face, it seemed like hours rather than minutes. He reached for her hand and squeezed it gently. Delaney would never forget the warmth, the shape and the feel of that hand. The strength, despite his weakened condition. She'd held onto that hand her entire life, and she didn't know what she'd do if there came a day when she couldn't.

"What do you say?" His blue eyes probed hers deeply.

She wished the twins and Hank were here. It was a decision she didn't want to make alone. "I don't understand all this medical jargon, Daddy, but I know I don't want you to die—" She choked on the last word and swallowed hard. She swatted at a blur of tears and said fiercely, "I'm going to find a way to make Eli Stark pay for this."

Alarm flashed in his eyes. "Don't do something brash, Delaney. Stark isn't one to take lightly."

"I know, but maybe he's misjudged us McCalls, too, and just because four of us are female."

"Promise me you'll be careful."

She couldn't do that, so she said, "The doc's waiting for your consent to operate."

She saw the uncertainty in his eyes and finally the capitulation. "I don't want to have to do this, but I guess I have no choice if there's any chance at all that she might be able to save my life."

116

His grip tightened on Delaney's hand. "If I make it through this, I won't be going anywhere for a while. You girls need to get on over to Virginia City where you'll be safe. I'm in as good of hands as I'm likely to get."

"We won't leave you here. You'd be a sitting duck for Stark."

His tone hardened. "If you won't go, then I'll get on Old Dan and finish taking you there myself."

Delaney had the notion that she'd do whatever she saw fit to do, and, sure enough, he saw that belligerent set to her jaw and the stubborn look in her eyes. "Don't go against me on this, Delaney. Promise me that as soon as the operation is over, and she doesn't need you anymore, that you'll head out of here. Unless I die. Then you'll have to bury me, I reckon."

"You're not going to die."

Delaney looked at him long and hard, wondering if it would be the last time she saw him alive. "I hope Stark burns in hell for tearing up our lives like this."

"Delaney . . . promise."

She wanted to cry. She could deal with a god-awful lot, but not something that might take her father from her forever. "All right, Daddy. I promise. But I don't believe in us splitting up for any reason. You always said—"

"I know what I said about strength in numbers and how a family should always stick together. But sometimes there comes a time when each of us has to go our own way."

"We'll stay together," she said stubbornly. "I'll make sure of that."

He didn't have the strength to continue. "I've got one more favor, Delaney."

"I'm listening." But she was wary of making another promise she might not be able to keep.

"Take Old Dan. If Stark spots him over at the livery, he'll

know I'm around. Besides, if something should happen, I don't want anybody to have him but you girls. And something else." He reached into his inside vest pocket and pulled out the old daguerreotype of Delaney's mother. He looked at it for a long moment then handed it to her with an unsteady hand. "This is yours. I always intended on giving it to you since you never knew your mother."

Delaney reflexively tried to stop a sob welling up in her throat as her hand closed over thes photograph. She wanted to tell him he was going to live through this, that everything would be all right, but all she could do was nod and choke back burning tears.

Believing he had all his affairs in order, Luke McCall said, "Okay, tell the doctor I'm ready."

Sam Saxton allowed his horse a leisurely pace down the main street of Dutch Flat, but beneath the brim of his hat his eyes missed nothing that went on around him. Down the street he spotted the big muscled gray that Luke McCall rode and the buckskin that belonged to the black-haired girl. They were hitched in front of Richman's General Store, and right next to it was a doctor's office. It was a good guess they were in the latter.

He drew rein at the saloon across the street. He could use a shot of good whiskey while he waited. He was confident now that the McCalls were headed into Nevada. Probably Virginia City. It was the only smart thing to do. But he wasn't in a hurry to haul them in. He had two months to collect them and he had some plans for that dark-haired girl. She stirred his blood.

He sauntered into the saloon and up to the bar. He bought a bottle and ignored the barkeeper's curious eyes as he palmed both it and a shot glass and made his way to the empty table by the window. It offered a good view of the doctor's office and the two horses. He thought the McCalls ought to ride less conspicuous mounts. Most outlaws wouldn't ride horses that drew attention or were easily remembered. It seemed to be one more indication that Eli Stark had his own side to this story, and it wasn't necessarily the truthful one.

Nobody bothered Sam as he took his position by the window, but then nobody ever bothered him. Most people took one look at him and cut him a wide swath. It suited him.

He took the whiskey slowly, but the bottle was a third gone by the time darkness settled over the town and the lamplighter started his corner to corner ritual, illuminating the streets. When the spindly-legged man had six lamps lit, Sam saw movement across the street.

The dark-haired girl came out of the doctor's office alone and stood for a moment in the gathering darkness. Had her father died? She paused at the edge of the boardwalk and glanced up and down the street.

She went into the general store again, then went to two other general stores, carrying bundles from all three. She managed it just before they all turned their "closed" signs to the window. Then she untied both horses, swung into the saddle, and led the gray. She headed out of town on a trot, glancing over her shoulder at the doctor's office. A last good-bye? Or did she suspect she was being followed?

He left the whiskey bottle on the table and swiftly exited the saloon.

Delaney left Dutch Flat quickly, frightened by the sight of the horse tied in front of the Blackjack Saloon. She might forget a name, or even a face, but she never forgot a horse. It was too coincidental that the stranger they'd run into back in the Diablos, and then seen in Sacramento, would now be in Dutch Flat. He might be the handsomest man she'd ever seen, but she hadn't trusted his motives then. Seeing him here only made her more suspicious of his intentions.

She trotted Buck past the street lamps and the buildings, then into the encroaching darkness for a quarter of a mile before skirting the fires and lanterns of the emigrants. They watched her passage. She knew they would remember her as having gone into town with a companion and coming back leading Old Dan. Nobody forgot Old Dan.

She wasn't keen on leaving her father alone, but she'd made that promise. Besides, the twins and Hank would be wondering what was keeping them, and thinking the worst. She was surprised they hadn't already ridden into town, searching for them, and she suddenly hoped something hadn't befallen them. She stepped up the buckskin's pace to a trot.

When she rode into camp, Hank was saddling up. The three of them swarmed around her.

"Where's Daddy?" they chorused in frightened unison.

Delaney swung to the ground and handed Old Dan's reins to Hank. While she unsaddled her buckskin, she told them what had transpired.

"He was still alive when I left," she concluded morosely. "The lady doctor seemed pleased with all her clipping and stitching and the removal of the bullet. She said the bullet hadn't messed his insides up too much, but she wouldn't guarantee anything. Said time would tell. She told me to go to the hotel and get some rest. She doesn't know who we are or anything. Daddy told her our name was Taylor."

"How long is he going to be laid up?"

"The doc said if he lives he couldn't do any riding for at least a month. I think she saw Daddy as somebody who was going to die anyway, so she figured she might as well practice on him."

"Do you think she'll take good care of him?"

"If she wants to prove her surgery is successful, she had darn well better take good care of him. But I did notice one thing. She seemed a little taken with him. Course, most women are."

Delaney told them what their father had made her promise. Then she told them about the horse that she believed belonged to the stranger.

"It was coming dark," Brett countered. "Maybe you were mistaken."

Delaney squatted in front of the fire and dished up a plateful of the chipped beef Hank had prepared. "I don't think so."

"It's too much of a coincidence."

"Do you think he's following us?"

She toyed with the food on her plate, not really having an appetite. "Could be. But why? If he was a bounty hunter, he could have walked right into that doctor's office and gotten two of us then."

"He could have gotten three of us back in the Diablos."

"He said he was wanting to do some gold mining. Maybe it *is* just coincidence that he's going the same way we are," Andy said hopefully.

A bad feeling washed over Delaney. She stood up and looked back through the darkness toward town. The others saw the look in her eye and tensed. Her premonitions had a tendency to come true too many times to ignore.

"What is it, Delaney?"

"What if he went into the doctor's office and finished Daddy off?" The food lost its appeal and she set it aside.

Simultaneously, they all came to their feet.

"Let's get this fire doused and get into town," Hank said.

They all knew that if the stranger had been there to kill Luke McCall, it was too late to stop him.

Sam Saxton touched the ashes of the campfire. They were still warm, almost hot. He lifted his head and glanced around the camp. They'd lit out of here fast, gathered everything up and gone. Had they known he was on their trail? He cursed. He wasn't going to be able to track them in the dark.

He lit a candle from his pack and nosed around to see if he could see which direction they'd taken, but there were too many tracks confusing the sign. He wondered if they had done it on purpose to throw off any pursuers.

He built another fire on the warm ashes and settled into his blankets. Sooner or later, the daughters of Luke McCall were going to have to sleep.

CHAPTER ELEVEN

LEADIN' OLD DAN

Hank and the twins stayed hidden while Delaney checked on their father again. She was thankful to find him still alive, and to find the stranger, who'd been at the saloon, apparently gone about his own business.

Doc Hogan, true to her word, hovered protectively over Luke. Delaney took her father's hand. Although he wasn't riding at top speed, he had enough strength to squeeze back.

"Do as I told you, Delaney. I'll catch up soon as I can."

"We don't want to leave you, Daddy."

"I know, but you have to this time."

Later, after Delaney had kissed his cheek and told him good-bye, she hurried out into the darkness to cover her tears.

The climb into the Sierra Nevadas slowed their flight. Occasionally, they could see for miles behind them at the emigrant trail, but never once did they see anybody who might be following them.

They were the only people heading into the mountains. Everyone else was hurrying for California, including one emigrant train and a dozen riders. Before the emigrants spotted them, the McCalls moved off the trail and hid in the thick timber until the trail was clear again. They didn't want anybody, if questioned by Stark, to be able to say they'd seen the four of them heading over the pass.

Delaney noted the silence of the mountains when it started to snow on the third day out. They had all felt it coming. Saw it coming. The temperature dropped and the clouds appeared out of nowhere, sinking into the ravines and blotting out the sky and the mountain peaks. The snow fell lightly at first, but soon the flakes had puffed up to the size of nickels and were wet and heavy and collected rapidly on the pine boughs, the horses' manes, and the girls' shoulders. If there was a bird or an animal lurking in the protection of those silent green sentinels, they didn't see it.

"What I wouldn't give for some sand between my toes," Brett jested, but there was worry in her eyes as she surveyed their unfamiliar surroundings. If it hadn't been for the emigrant trail carved through the trees, they'd have been lost.

Nobody responded to Brett because there was something more frightening about breaking the silence than the silence itself.

Toward evening they came to a lake which they surmised was the notorious Donner Lake. They pulled rein to stare down at its icy water reflecting the gray of the sky. Delaney couldn't feel her toes so she got down from the saddle to get circulation in them again, but the snow made her boots wetter and her feet colder.

She had never been this cold. It was a cold that chilled to the bone; a cold that could kill in a matter of hours. If they died, nobody would find their bones until spring. Maybe not even then if the wolves and other wild animals found them first.

"This place gives me the jitters," Andy said.

"Knowing that Donner bunch resorted to popping each other into their stewing kettles doesn't help any," Delaney replied.

"Who knows, maybe their spirits are still hanging around, watching us." A chill raced visibly through Andy's slender frame. "Maybe they're still hungry."

A sudden soughing, like the voices of the dead, filtered through the pines and drew the girls' eyes upward. The snow wasn't coming straight down anymore, but blowing horizontally.

"It'll be dark soon," Hank said. "We need to find shelter for the night."

Delaney eyes roamed the mountains, reflecting the uneasiness they all felt about the ominous quality of the storm. Winter would be setting in soon. Was this the beginning? "We've been spoiled out on the coast. The most we've ever had to deal with was some rain."

Hank tugged her hat down tighter onto her head and pulled her hair from the plait to protect her neck and ears from the cold. "Let's get down off this mountain as fast as we can. I don't think I could eat one of you girls no matter how hungry I got."

"That's a comforting thought." Brett leaned forward in the saddle and led the way.

They set up camp near the lower end of the lake. Three inches of snow had fallen and no end appeared to be in sight. They built a shelter on the backside of an outcropping of granite, shaping it with sticks and pine boughs and hoping the wind wouldn't get strong enough to bring it down around their ears. They put their horses behind some brush and in some thick trees not far away, giving them as much protection as possible.

They managed to get a fire going on the edge of the shelter, then huddled shoulder to shoulder, hands and toes extended toward the flame. They rationed the dried fruit, jerky, coffee, and hardtack that Delaney had bought in town.

When their bellies were semi-full they curled up close together, piling every blanket they had on top of them.

"I swear, it's colder than hell on the stoker's holiday," Hank said, trying to keep the blankets down around her shoulders.

Delaney stared into the fire, her teeth chattering. Her toes were numb and she feared they might freeze and rot and fall off. She remembered the way her father's hand had been so warm when she'd left him, and she wondered if it still was. She figured she wouldn't be so scared and lost if he was with them.

"If Daddy dies, we won't even know it," she said solemnly.

"He isn't going to die," Brett snapped, suddenly yanking at the blankets and uncovering Delaney who was on the opposite outside edge of their makeshift bed.

That flared Delaney's temper and she yanked back. "All you ever think about is covering your own rear end, Brett. Let me have some of the covers!"

"I'm on the windward side, you little heathen. The wind is blowing right up my back." The covers slid over to Brett's side again.

"Damn-blast it, Brett!" Delaney hauled the blankets back.

"The two of you—stop!" Hank, in the middle with Andy, sat up. "You keep yanking the covers back and forth and you'll have them torn in half."

"Maybe if Brett didn't have such a big derriere, she wouldn't have such a hard time covering it."

Brett came up off the bed and was about to clamber over the top of Hank and Andy to get to Delaney when the two of them caught her shoulders and forced her back down.

"Let's straighten out the covers and start over," Hank said, but her tone warned that she was on the very edge of her good humor. "Delaney and Brett can sleep on the outside for a couple of hours, then Andy and I will trade you off."

Brett and Delaney glared at each other. "I'll sleep on the outside all night," Delaney declared. "It beats rubbing shoulders with her."

Brett's eyes flashed. "That's the best news I've heard all day."

Finally they settled down and allowed Hank and Andy to spread the blankets equally again. They still didn't quite reach from side to side, so Brett and Delaney used the horse blankets to cover the edges.

"Now, are we all happy?" Hank's tone warned that the answer had better be a positive one.

"As happy as pigs in shit," Delaney retorted.

Brett tried to get comfortable on the ground that was not only hard as a rock but not exactly flat either. "I think we're going to die in this godforsaken place. It irks me to no end because I wanted to see Paris."

Andy's soft voice drifted out into the darkness. "If we do —die—do you think Daddy will know? I've heard of people who can sense when death or bad things befall the people they love. They get a sudden vision or a feeling that tells them. I even had a friend in school who said the ghost of her mother came to her. Later, after she'd received word that her mother had died, she returned home and learned that her mother *had* died exactly when she'd seen her ghost."

"That's bizarre," Brett said. "I wonder if she was lying."

"No, I don't think so."

They lapsed into silence, closing their eyes and trying to sleep, but it was so cold. What if they did die, and all because Eli Stark wanted something he couldn't have?

The raw feeling of despair lodged in Delaney's gut. She thought of her father and tried to will him to stay alive. She took her harmonica from her pack and played a mournful song. It had no name that she knew of. It was just something she'd heard an old Mexican strumming on his guitar years ago in the streets of Monterey. If somebody was after them, it would be a dead giveaway to their location, but her sisters seemed to relish the comfort of the music and didn't ask her to stop.

Without Daddy, the family circle was broken. Even though the four of them were as tight as tenpenny nails in a two-cent tin, Delaney could feel the gap widen where he'd been. She feared he'd never be there again to fill that gap, and then the circle would become weak and crumble and they would all go flying off in different directions. All because of Eli Stark.

The snow and these mountains frightened her, but not nearly as much as that weakening circle. She wanted to go back—just a couple of weeks would do. But she was on a one-way course, headed down a dark, unknown trail that was being obliterated by snow. The future stretched as uncertain as that trail, and she wished she could stay in this pine bough shelter forever so she wouldn't have to face it.

By midnight the storm had worsened. Delaney awoke with a start. The dream had been too real. Daddy had died and his spirit had floated out over the mountains, telling them good-bye.

No, it's just all that talk. It isn't real.

She heard the wind outside their pathetic shelter, howling and blowing snow. The fire had burned down to coals, but there was enough light left from it that she could see the snow sifting onto their blankets. The pine boughs shook and the sticks they'd used to prop them up with looked none too sturdy. If the snow was blowing over the granite outcropping, it would be piling up on their pine bough shelter. The whole thing might collapse and bury them.

And it was cold. So cold.

She slid carefully from under the blankets and put more sticks on the fire. She waited until the wood caught and then she added some larger pieces. It was probably fifteen or twenty minutes before she returned to the relative warmth of the bed.

"I'll trade you places," Hank whispered.

"No, I'll be all right," Delaney assured her, returning to her original spot on the outside. "I'm sorry I woke you."

"I wasn't asleep. It's too cold, and I was worried about Daddy."

Delaney considered telling Hank about the dream and how real it had seemed, but she decided against it. She remembered that old wives' tale that if you told a dream before breakfast it would come true.

"Wouldn't it be ironic," Hank whispered, "if we died right here in this pine hut after Daddy's the one who got shot?"

"Yeah, and especially after he sent us this way to keep us safe."

"Word is bound to get back to him about this snowstorm blocking off the pass. He'll be worried."

"Maybe we ought to try to get word to him—if we make it through, that is."

"I don't know, Delaney. We can't risk letting anybody know where we are."

"We've got to get this mess straightened out, Hank. We can't spend the rest of our lives on the run."

"I guess I really am an outlaw. It doesn't seem real."

"You killed those two men defending Daddy. You're not a murderer."

Hank didn't reply and Delaney continued, "Are you going to be all right, sis?"

Hank released a long sigh. "Who has the luxury of feeling

sorry for themselves? At least we've got each other, we're not having to face this ordeal alone."

"Maybe Daddy will get this cleared up when he recovers. Write a letter to the governor or maybe the U.S. Marshal. Maybe he'll hire a good lawyer or something."

The wind howled louder in the silence that fell between them. Delaney said, "The horses are miserable. There's not a blade of grass for them to eat, and we might have days before we're out of these mountains. I wish we had some idea just how far it is."

"I hear it's about a hundred miles across. Of course I don't know where that starts and where it ends and we're into it quite a distance. Maybe we'll find some southerly facing slopes where the wind has blown the snow clear and exposed some grass."

Their talking woke up the twins, but they joined the conversation. "What are we going to do to make a living when we get to Virginia City?" Brett said. "The only thing we know to do is chase mustangs."

"I've been thinking about it," Andy answered. "I figure we could get typical female jobs that won't put enough bread on the table to keep us from starving, or we can set up our own business."

Brett propped herself up on one elbow and peered at her twin from over the top of Hank. "We're not without education, but you need capital to set up a business, and we don't have a whole lot with us. We may have to look for financing, or a partner with plush pockets."

Personally, all Delaney wanted to do was chase mustangs. This talk of going into business sounded pretty dull to her. "Do they have mustangs in Nevada? We could do that. Besides, nobody in Nevada has ever heard of the McCalls."

Brett was quick to refute her suggestion, but Brett's point

was valid. "Four women chasing mustangs would be a dead giveaway to any bounty hunter looking for us, Delaney. Let's hear Andy's idea."

"Actually, I was thinking of a card house," Andy eagerly supplied. "It would bring in the money faster than anything I can think of, especially in a mining town like Virginia City. Why, that's about all those miners do is drink and gamble."

"And whore," Delaney put in.

"Well, we won't be offering that particular service."

"Will they keep coming if we don't?"

"They won't be able to resist four beautiful, intelligent women. You'll have to wear a dress, though, Delaney."

Delaney wasn't happy to hear that. Dresses meant corsets, and she couldn't think of a thing worse than a corset.

"Do we have to wear those floozy ones like whores wear?"

"No. We'll dress like ladies and act like ladies. That way we'll be treated like ladies."

"Won't we draw less attention to ourselves if we find a less conspicuous job?" Delaney was still dubious about the whole idea. She felt safer horseback. Besides, cards bored her to tears after a short while and she wasn't as good at it as Andy.

"We'll change our names." Andy had obviously given it considerable thought. "We won't admit to being sisters, well, except for me and Brett. If any man is looking for the faces on that Wanted poster, he won't see them in us when we've got ourselves all feathered out. The Wanted poster makes no reference to twins so that shouldn't give us away."

They finally decided it sounded like the only way to make a lot of money in a short span of time. Better that than scrubbing clothes or floors or wearing themselves out over a hot stove in a two-bit restaurant. If the Wanted posters and the bounty hunters found their way to Virginia City, living fast and running hard was going to become a way of life and they'd need money—a lot of it.

They settled back into their blankets, but Delaney was still awake when the wind quit just before dawn. At least the storm was over. If it had dragged on, their chances of reaching the other side alive would have been dramatically reduced.

Suddenly she bolted upright, flaring her nostrils and breathing the cold mountain air into her lungs.

Slowly she reached for her .44.

Someone was out there. And there was no mistaking the smell of his tobacco.

CHAPTER TWELVE

HIGH-HEADED

It was the stranger from the Diablos, just as Delaney had suspected. There he sat, as pretty as you please, not thirty feet away, puffing a cheroot and begging a small fire to burn. A thick stand of brush blocked the wind from his back. A sheet of gutta-percha protected him from the frozen ground. Another piece covered his shoulders in an inadequate attempt to keep a couple of wool blankets dry. It gave her considerable satisfaction to note that he looked as cold and miserable as the four of them were.

She said, "I'd advise you not to move, mister, unless you want your next step to be through the Pearly Gates."

The stranger jerked his head up like a startled buck deer and found himself staring down the barrels of four Colt revolvers.

"Remove your sidearm and toss it aside," Delaney ordered.

He clearly didn't like that suggestion. "There's a foot of snow out here, ma'am. I'll never see it again if I do that."

"That's not a big concern of mine. Just do it."

His back stiffened. "I've done nothing to threaten you. And I'm more than a little partial to this .44. Having it close at hand—so to speak—might mean the difference between life and death in these mountains."

Delaney felt flustered and furious. For him to attempt in-

133

subordination in the face of her "persuader" was pushing his luck too far.

"I can respect that direction of thought, mister," she said. "I know the worth of a good six-shooter, so we'll make a compromise. You *gently* pull that iron from its holster with two fingers. Act like it's the far end of a hot poker, then hand it over to my sister here." She nodded toward Hank, who was crouching next to her. "If you do that, you've got a fair to middlin' chance of seeing your next birthday."

The man did some more grumbling, this time about being treated like a common criminal, but he relented and the weapon exchange went smoothly.

"Now, get your tongue to flapping," Delaney ordered, feeling safer now. "You've got some explaining to do."

He tried to look innocent. "I don't know what you mean, ma'am."

"Sure you do. Don't you think it's a bit coincidental that everywhere we turn, you just happen to be there."

That lit his lantern. He half-smiled. "Well, yeah, I guess it is coincidental, but that's all it is. I'm not following you, if that's what you're implying. I decided to see what the hullabaloo was over at the Comstock diggings. Last I heard, you all were tracking down some mares stolen by a renegade stallion. Don't tell me you followed him and his band all this way?"

His eyes needled; he knew better.

How were they going to walk their way around this one?

Brett sauntered—if one can saunter in a foot of snow—to the foreground. "That stallion took our profits to hell and gone. So we just turned our ponies around and headed north. Once we got the wind beneath our wings, we let it carry us."

"This is a hell of a place to land."

His quick wit, under the circumstances, wasn't expected or appreciated. "We don't dispute that," Andy stepped into the middle. "But who figured it would dump this much snow in October?"

"Obviously not the four of you."

"You're really pushing your luck, mister," Brett warned.

Delaney sensed he believed them about as much as they believed him, but all the yarns, on both sides, eased the tension.

"Can I have my sidearm back now?"

Hank slid the revolver into her belt. "You know what happens to a horse that holds his head too high."

He shrugged. "It was worth a try."

Hank lashed him with disdainful eyes. "It looks like you'll be traveling the rest of the way to Virginia City with us, so we'll just hold onto your revolver and that rifle in your saddle scabbard until we part company in that fair city. Oh, and we'd appreciate you turning over all your ammunition too."

"And your hide-out weapons," Delaney added.

The stranger obeyed, giving them his ammunition, but reminded them he didn't have any weapons hidden on his person. He pulled his gutta-percha a little tighter around his shoulders. "I just hope you ladies can hit what you're aiming at. I don't hanker starving to death."

"If we get too hungry," Andy quipped, "we'll just eat *you*. It wouldn't be the first time it's happened here in the Sierras."

There wasn't much left to be said, and they were all anxious to put some miles behind them. They gave the horses a portion of the oats Delaney had bought at the general store. Delaney even gave a handful to the stranger's bay because she felt sorry for him—the bay, not the stranger. They satisfied their own hunger with more jerky, coffee, and hardtack.

While Delaney saddled her buckskin, she kept an eye on the stranger. There was still the matter of that particular brand of tobacco, the same she'd smelled in the *cabaña*. Of course it might only be another coincidence, and if she mentioned it, it would blow the lid off their own tall tale and lay them bare. If this stranger *was* a bounty hunter, he would have captured the four of them in their bed last night. He could have captured two of them in the Diablos, and two of them at Dutch Flat. One thing was still bothering her.

"Why did you camp right next to us and not wake us?" She pinned him with a demanding gaze.

He didn't so much as bat a black-fringed eyelash. "You can't blame me for wanting company during that snowstorm. I didn't wake you because I figured morning would be soon enough for introductions."

"Don't go on a campaign against the truth for my benefit."

"You know, lady, you're about as pleasant as a boot full of barbed wire."

"We didn't ask you here. Don't forget that."

As Delaney turned away from him and swung into her cold saddle, she was thinking that if the stranger was any kind of man at all—and he looked to be—he might just come in handy before this journey was over.

Eli Stark slogged his way through the muddy main street of Nevada City. After three days of searching every gold town in the Grass Valley area, he had finally come to the conclusion that the kid at the Auburn livery had given him bum information about the direction Saxton had gone. That meant that if Saxton was still on the trail of the McCalls, then they had probably taken the road to Emigrant Gap instead of Grass Valley. That also meant that their destination had either been Gold Run or Dutch Flat. Hell, they might even have been foolish enough to head over the mountains to Virginia City.

He saw an old-timer sitting out of the rain on the board-walk in front of the Gold Pan Saloon. He was bundled up for the weather and reading a newspaper. Eli drew rein in front of him. The old man looked up over the top of small spectacles; his thorough scrutiny didn't miss the badge Eli had trans-ferred to the lapel of his oilskin. If he wasn't mistaken, Eli saw a flash of contempt before the man returned his attention to his newspaper.

"Hello there." Eli's friendly greeting drew the old-timer's eyes from the newsprint again. "I was wondering if you could help me. I'm looking for a band of five outlaws, and a man who would be following them, a bounty hunter."

The old man shook his newspaper a little as if to keep the pages from collapsing in the dampness, but Eli took it more as a movement of aggravation at having been disturbed. "I see lots of people coming and going in this town, marshal, but they never stop to tell me whether they're outlaws *or* bounty hunters."

Eli bridled his temper. "The outlaws are a father and his four daughters. The latter are dressed like men."

That lifted the old man's eyebrows. "Female outlaws? Now, ain't that fascinating. What did they do anyway?"

"Stole some horses and murdered three men, last count."

The old man looked hard at him, and Eli had the feeling he wasn't necessarily inclined to believe him. "What kind of horses were they riding? I'd probably remember the horses before I would the people."

"The man is riding a big gray. One of the girls is on a buck-skin, another on a black, and two rode sorrels. The man who's following them is riding a blood bay. I've got to find them before he does. He's a bloodthirsty sonofabitch who's liable to shoot first and ask questions later."

The old man was indifferent to Eli's problems. He spat tobacco out into the street. "I hate to disappoint you, marshal, but I'm afraid I can't be of any help."

Disappointed, Eli hunched down in his oilskin, feeling the chill settle into his bones. "Then could you recommend a place where I can get a warm room, a bottle of Red Eye, and maybe somebody who would be of some help."

The old man was unmoved by Stark's sharp tongue. "Place across the street will give you the first two, I reckon."

Eli reined his horse around without so much as a thank you. The animal was tired and hungry and would have preferred to stay put, but Eli hit him with the ends of his long reins until he turned and crossed the street. At the hotel, he stopped close to the boardwalk so he could swing from the saddle without stepping in the mud.

As he looped his reins around the hitching rail, the mighty presence of the Sierras drew his attention. Snow was falling up there. If that was where they'd headed then they wouldn't have to worry about their back trail because he wasn't about to head into those mountains this time of the year. Not even Henrietta McCall and a twenty-six-year-old vendetta was worth dying for.

As for Saxton, if the bounty hunter had wanted his money bad enough to follow them, then he could die right along with them. Not many people made it out of those mountains this time of the year, especially people who were heading into them without adequate supplies and protection.

Actually, he wasn't all that concerned. He didn't believe that Luke McCall would leave California. He had probably headed south to familiar territory and a warmer climate. McCall would keep trying to get his name cleared and the charges dropped. If that happened, Eli was bound to hear about it. Whatever it had started out as, it didn't matter now.

Nobody made a laughingstock out of Eli Stark and got away with it.

They found the trail only by the swath that the emigrants had cut though the trees. It had become well-traveled since 1845, nearly twenty years ago, but the fresh snow made the going slow and tiring for the horses. The girls and the stranger—who told them his name was Sam Saxton—took turns in the lead, breaking trail. It kept them from over-working any one horse. They also took turns riding Old Dan. He was big and strong and liked being in the lead. He was un-daunted by the snow.

Old Dan particularly took a liking to Sam. It irked Delaney. "He isn't Daddy, for Pete's sake," she grumbled to Hank when Sam took the lead.

"No, but Dan is used to a man handling him, and Saxton's got that special touch, like Daddy, that horses seem to re-spond to. I think Old Dan misses Daddy."

Delaney wouldn't be pacified. "He could take up with one of us. Talk about being disloyal."

Hank grinned. "Don't take it personal, Delaney. Daddy says that animals can sense the good and bad in people better than people can. You were probably about five years old when we had that old dog, Skeeter. There were times when a stranger would come around the *cabaña* and Skeeter wouldn't let that person within a hundred feet of the house and us girls. Other times, he'd see somebody coming, sniff 'em out, and flop back on the porch."

"Well, Old Dan might trust Saxton, but I don't. It's some-thing in his eyes. He's hiding something."

"Aren't we all? But the way I see it is if he can help us get out of these mountains alive, we'll deal with who and what he is when we reach Virginia City. Don't worry." Hank gave her an understanding look.

Despite their efforts, the animals soon showed signs of weakening from laboring through the snow with little nourishment. The girls dished out the last of the oats and plodded on. Once they reached the lower elevations, the horses would have all the grass they wanted. Saxton assured them it wasn't far.

"Thought you hadn't been in this country before," Delaney goaded.

"Some boys over in a saloon in Dutch Flat gave me good directions."

Delaney thought he was stretching the truth again. At least the sun was shining now and the temperature had risen. The only trace of the storm was the snow it had left behind. With the warmth of a new day at her back, Delaney might have enjoyed the snow and the awesome majesty of the Sierras had it not been for the circumstances—and if their father had been with them.

The five of them seemed to be alone in the mountains; apparently the last of the emigrants had already crossed. They stopped the next night in a place where some tall, dry grass was exposed on a southerly-facing hill and the horses were able to paw down further and get a fair amount to fill their bellies. That evening, Delaney saw a snowshoe rabbit and shot it with her .44. Hank roasted it on a spit and Sam proclaimed it had to be the best meal he'd ever eaten. Delaney told him that a piece of hardtack would look good to a starving man.

He disputed everything she said, including that. "Only if you've got a cup of black coffee to soak it in, ma'am."

She detested him calling her "ma'am." It made her feel too much like a woman, and too much aware that he was a man. She detested, too, the unfamiliar feelings his nearness stirred.

140

When they reached the lower elevation, the snow line ended abruptly, but the cold nights spent crossing the Sierras were taking their toll on Sam Saxton. The girls had had the luxury of being able to sleep together at night, keeping each other warm. Saxton had had to sleep alone, and the chill had settled deep inside him. Delaney was the first to notice the fever in his eyes.

Over a mid-day meal of more jerky and hardtack, she gave him a good measure from her position on a boulder, ten feet away. "You look like you're coming down with a sickness, Saxton."

Her observation surprised him. "I'm feeling a little rough, but I'll be all right. We'll be in Virginia City soon enough."

"There's nothing we can do for you out here anyway, I suppose."

Still she worried, despite her nonchalance. What if he got sick and died? Of course, on the other hand, it might solve some problems. The man could cause them a lot of trouble once they reached civilization. He knew they were sisters and it could mess up their plan to start a gambling house using different names. At least Brett had been quick to tell him that their last name was Taylor.

As they headed out of the mountains, though, it was Luke McCall who captured Delaney's thoughts. She had the peculiar notion that he was back there, trying to catch up. She looked over her shoulder more than once but saw nothing except the calm of the snow draped like a lady's mantle on the boughs of the pines. It was a crazy notion because he couldn't possibly ride until he was healed. That is, if he was even still alive.

"Is something wrong, Delaney?" Hank followed her worried gaze, soaking up everything they were leaving behind—their lives, their dreams.

141

"We'll probably never see the other side of these mountains again, will we?" Delaney's heart felt like ten tons of lead. "*Or* Daddy. You know, Hank, I'm really going to see Eli Stark in his grave for doing this to us."

"We just have to go on, sis. We can't dwell on what was. We're starting new lives now, whether we want to or not."

"It's one of those things we've been telling you about all along, Delaney," Brett inserted. "You have to learn to adjust to life's changes."

"I don't think this is exactly what you had in mind."

Brett gathered her reins. "No, but we'll call it progress and make it work to our advantage."

Brett took the lead, as she usually did. Delaney stayed behind, being the last to turn her buckskin into the snowy path. She watched her sisters' backs, and Saxton's. If her eyes frequently lingered on Sam's broad back, who was there to notice?

The five of them were all so inconsequential in this land of towering mountains, towering trees and sky, towering silence. The silence was all around them. Silence up ahead. Silence behind. It soaked into Delaney, clear to her bones. Clear to her heart. With it came an emptiness like nothing she had felt before . . . and prayed she would never feel again.

CHAPTER THIRTEEN

GROUND-HITCHED

Delaney halted the buckskin alongside her sisters and Sam. She leveled her eyes on Virginia City. Without stretching the truth, that pyramid of civilization clinging to the barren side of Mount Davidson, gray and cold in winter's preface, brought on a twinge of despair. Her sisters' faces mirrored her disappointment. Sam was clearly too sick to care.

"This is what we rode hundreds of miles for?" Brett's voice lifted in dismay. "My God, there's not a tree in sight."

Delaney slouched deeper in the saddle, feeling very weary. "Who would have ever dreamed that the Comstock Lode was under that ugly lump of sagebrush and rock?"

"It's prosperous. That's all that matters," Andy said optimistically.

Hank, too, attempted the positive. "Maybe it looks better in the spring. Besides, it'll give us what we need: food, shelter, and a doctor for Sam."

Delaney looked over at Saxton barely sticking to his saddle. She hated to admit it—and wouldn't have—but she had grown partial to him. She said, "I don't know if a doctor is going to do him much good. He looks like a gutted coyote."

She said it with nonchalance, but she decided she probably *would* be upset if he died.

"I'm going to be fine. You all quit worrying about me," he

managed before falling into a fit of coughing.

"Who's worrying, Saxton? It's not like you're kin."

They paused on the outskirts of town, surveying the drab buildings nestled against the gray hills. Smoke and steam from the mines drifted up into the quiet air and hung like a pall over the city. The mines and hoisting works were side by side with homes and businesses, gripping the mountainside in tiers with what had to be some pretty healthy claws. There seemed no rhyme or reason to the layout. If there was a boardwalk anywhere in the city, it was bound to be mighty lonesome. Brett wouldn't be doing much promenading in silk dresses down those streets.

By now Saxton knew of their plans to open up a gambling house. "You know, ladies, I could use a job and you'll be needing a bartender. I didn't come to Virginia City to go underground."

Delaney studied him thoroughly, as she had done often since he'd joined them in the Sierras. "Why don't you want to go down into the mines, Saxton? Do you have claustrophobia? Or just a streak of yellow?"

He laughed. "How'd you guess?"

"Which one?"

"A healthy dose of both. I was down in a mine once. That was enough."

"Well, we're going to have to discuss this." Hank's tone insinuated that they'd like to do so in private.

"I'll ride up the road a stretch," he offered.

They debated for ten minutes and finally decided it might work better for them to have a man along. However, if they didn't find him a doctor, they'd be putting him in a pine box instead of behind a bar.

With the girls still dressed in their manly attire, they went virtually unnoticed into the city of twenty thousand and easily found a place to stay. It wasn't the best hotel in town, but neither was it the worst. Delaney volunteered to go inside with Sam while the others stayed with the horses and gear. They got two rooms. Delaney signed in under the alias of L. Taylor. But she doubted the desk clerk would have remembered her anyway. He had his nose stuck in one of those new dime novels that had found its way west. He didn't even look up.

Delaney handed the pen to Sam and noticed how hot his skin was when his hand brushed hers. One look at him told her he was so weak he could barely stand.

"Would you have a doctor in the town?" he asked, scrawling a name that was completely illegible across the bottom.

The desk clerk looked up sharply. "Why? Do you have something contagious?"

Sam returned the pen to the center of the register. "My sister here's been having some female complaints."

The desk clerk's face flamed. So did Delaney's.

"Oh." Quickly the man returned his attention to his book, smoothing the pages anxiously. He refused to look at Delaney. She might as well have had the pox. "There are several doctors in town. The closest is just down the street. Dr. Fredericks. The women seem to . . . like him." He reached behind him, found the appropriate keys and thrust them at Sam.

"Much obliged." Sam took the keys then turned his back on Delaney's stunned face and gaping mouth and left the hotel.

Delaney was right on his heels. Outside, she grabbed his arm and whirled him around. He spun, nearly losing his balance and reached for her shoulder to steady himself. He might be sick, but at the moment Delaney wasn't brimming over with sympathy. "Telling that complete stranger that I was having . . . female troubles . . . was totally uncalled for, Sam Saxton. He'll probably think I'm in the family way or . . . or something worse."

Sam was too sick to kick up much of a counter-attack. "It worked, didn't it? He put his nose right back in that book and got it out of our business, and I got the information I needed."

She turned to her sisters who were standing on the boardwalk listening to the exchange. "And even worse than that, he told the clerk I was his sister."

Then, back at Sam. "We're only giving you a job, Saxton. We're not taking you into the fold."

He ran a hand across his fevered face. "I know it's not what we agreed to, but it just came out. It seemed to make more sense for us to be family. Course, I guess I could have told him you were my wife. . . ."

Delaney blanched. "That'd be a cold day in—"

Hank laid a restraining hand on Delaney's arm. "Calm down, Delaney. Maybe it's not such a bad idea after all. Us being his sisters, that is."

There was a long silence while they all mulled it over. Finally Andy said, "I always wanted a big brother."

"Maybe it'll work to our benefit," Brett admitted.

"He'll be working with us anyway." Hank.

All eyes turned to Delaney. Hers locked with Sam's. The strand of tension that had been between them right from the beginning got a notch tighter. They'd all accepted him. All of them except Delaney.

"I see I'm outnumbered," she finally said. "You can be *their* brother, Sam. I've gotten along fine without one for nearly twenty years."

"Three sisters are probably more than enough anyway," he retaliated, reaching for his reins. "Now, if you all will excuse me, I'm going to ride down the street and see if I can find that doctor." As if on cue, he started coughing. It sounded like the prelude to a funeral.

His foot missed the stirrup and he weaved on his feet, gripping the saddle horn to steady himself. Brett and Andy, standing closest to him, reached out to help. On the second try, he managed to get himself in the saddle. The fever had deepened in his eyes since this morning and he appeared disoriented.

"Which way did the clerk say it was?"

"He didn't," Delaney replied.

Andy moved to her sorrel. "I think I'd better go along."

Hank nodded. "Go ahead. We'll get the rest of the horses to the livery."

Doc Fredericks advised chicken soup, lots of marshmallow tea, fresh garlic cooked into everything, and plenty of toddies.

"What are we warding off here?" Delaney demanded. "A cold, or vampires?"

Her sisters were fussing around Sam like mother hens, helping him out of his clothes. They stripped him down to his long-handled underwear, but he was too sick to care. He rolled over into bed and drew the covers to his chin.

"He doesn't have pneumonia," Andy explained to Delaney, "but the doctor says it could develop into that. He's running a high fever and we need to get the congestion in his lungs broken up. We need to go to that restaurant across the street and see if they'll cooperate with us on some special food for him."

Delaney, who'd been standing back watching the proceedings, settled into the only chair. "We don't all need to be running over there. You three go. I'll keep an eye on Saxton so if he dies I can tell you exactly when it happens."

"And relish every second of it," Sam mumbled from the bed.

That sounded like a plan, so Hank and the twins changed into skirts and left their revolvers behind, against their better judgment. Delaney waited until they'd left the room and closed the door. Then she poured a glass of cold water from the pitcher on the bureau. She sat on the edge of the bed. Saxton felt the mattress dip and lifted an eyelid, peering at her suspiciously.

"What's that? Poison?"

She ignored the remark. "There was an old *curandera* who lived down around where we used to live," she said. "Her name was Luz. She told us it means 'Mary of the Light.' Anyway, Luz said that when a body is burning up with fever, the patient should drink as much water and liquid as he can. It helps to wash the sickness out. Now, if you can sit up, drink this. It's water."

He eyed the liquid warily despite her assurances, but propped himself up on an elbow. "The way I feel, I guess it wouldn't matter if it was poison."

She clicked her tongue. "It *isn't* poison."

His hand closed around hers. His was still hot as fire and shaking like an aspen leaf in the wind. Together they got the glass to his lips. He drank every last drop then collapsed back onto the bed.

"Thanks, Delaney." He wiped his lips with the back of his hand. But before his hand had barely dropped back to his chest, he was asleep.

"You're welcome, Sam."

Delaney sat on the edge of the bed and took the opportunity to study him. Her head filled with all questions about who he was and why he had come to Virginia City. He'd told them earlier he was going to the gold fields, then he ends up here and says he doesn't want to go into the mines. It didn't make sense, and he wore that gun too easy to be a miner anyway.

She had to accept that he must not be one of Stark's men or he would have already had them in handcuffs. Unless he was waiting until he felt better. Wouldn't that be ironic if they doctored him back to health and then he turned out to be a stinking bounty hunter?

When she heard her sisters coming down the hall thirty minutes later, she quickly moved to the chair again. They didn't need to suspect her growing interest in a man she didn't trust.

CHAPTER FOURTEEN

A HANDFUL OF MANE

Beer 15 cents
Whiskey 2 bits
Poker, Red Dog, Faro, Blackjack

Sam stood back, hammer in hand, and looked at the sign next to the door with a definite degree of pride. "So, what do you think? Is it straight?"

The McCall sisters stood two on either side of him and cocked their heads this way and that until they concluded that he had it about as straight as he could get it.

While he had been sick abed, they'd found an old general store for rent and converted it into a gambling house. The place wasn't as big as the girls would have liked, but it had furnished living quarters on the second floor. There was a room on the ground floor for Sam. Delaney hadn't liked the idea of him staying there, but her sisters felt it would be good to have him there for protection.

"Besides," Brett said. "If he's supposed to be our brother, it would look pretty suspicious to everybody in town if he didn't stay here with us."

They had paid one month's rent, cleaned up the place, put in a makeshift bar, four card tables, acquired ten cases of various liquors, and painted the two signs. They'd told Sam they wanted to sound "more exotic" so from here on out he was to call them Rita, Brittany, Andrea, and Laney.

Sam hadn't questioned why they'd chosen to use different names. They gave him back his .44. He returned it to his hip and placed his rifle within easy access on the shelf under the bar. Delaney had finally decided he was harmless, except maybe to her heart.

They had made dresses and fancied them up with lace and passementerie. They had piled each other's hair up with pins, curls, and fancy combs. They had bought corsets and cinched them tight.

The repairs, purchases, clothing, and overhead for *The House of Cards* had left them with barely enough money to buy food and supplies. They were down to dimes, not dollars. Sam saw the situation and brought home a crate filled with everything from canned milk to peaches.

"We'll pay you back," they assured him.

Sam brushed it aside. "If you'll cook for me, we'll just call it even."

Everyone, except Delaney, hugged his neck. She saw no point in being too friendly. Getting too close to Sam Saxton made her about as jumpy as a jackrabbit in a den of wolves.

Her eyes traveled to the other sign above the door that identified the establishment as *The House of Cards*. She and Sam had painted the sign while he was recuperating. It was larger than the other one and spanned the front of the building. Its letters, painted in white and outlined in red and black—the colors of a deck of cards—leaped out at passersby. Some were already loitering around, waiting to see what the five of them were going to do next.

"It looks great, Sam," Hank said. "I don't see how you could get it any straighter."

"Well, ladies? Are you ready for business?"

Hank, Brett, and Andy couldn't think of anything they'd

forgotten. They turned to Delaney to get the final say.

Delaney likened this new enterprise to mustanging. It seemed the right time to grab mane and leap into the saddle. She had a niggling fear that somebody would recognize them as soon as those doors opened. With Sam around though, she couldn't voice that fear.

Thoughts flashed across her mind about Daddy. They'd been so busy these past couple of weeks, she'd hardly had time to think about him. If he was still alive, would he approve of their new enterprise? More than likely he'd tell them they had just set their own trap. Of course, she couldn't say that in front of Sam either.

She released an apprehensive sigh. "It's too late to turn back now. I guess we might as well do it."

As she led the way into *The House of Cards*, Delaney couldn't help wondering how long it would take before it tumbled. She would not have guessed it would take only eight hours.

The man stepped away from the door and stood for a moment, familiarizing himself with the layout of the establishment. Then he sauntered in, ordered whiskey, and leaned a hip against the bar.

Brett tried to keep her mind on the game of Blackjack she was dealing, but she felt the stranger's eyes perusing her and her sisters. She wondered if he was here by coincidence or intent.

There were four men at her table, all waiting for a young miner by the name of Max Henshaw to make up his mind if he wanted another card. His face screwed up and he floundered once again. Finally he caved in. "Oh, what the hell, Miss Brittany. Give me another one."

She said, "Are you sure, Max? You're sitting with seventeen."

"Don't get him going again," another miner at the table said. "Give the kid a card or we'll be here 'til Thanksgiving."

Max was trying hard to be decisive. "Okay. I'm sure. Give me the card, Miss Brittany. All I've got to lose is money."

Brett liked Max and sensed he was making a mistake. She already had most of his money. She reminded herself that they were in the business to make money, but she felt sorry for the kid. He wasn't old enough to use good judgment, and didn't.

A movement at the bar caught her eye. The stranger had left his position and was headed toward her table. He was lean, handsome, swarthy-complexioned, nattily dressed, but with the look of a drunk heading for trouble. He stopped behind Max, took him by the collar and firmly removed him from his chair. At the same time, he placed a twenty-dollar gold piece in his hand. "You were going to lose anyway, young man." He flashed the kid a white-toothed, feral grin. "Go on home to your mother."

"My mother's in Ohio, mister," Max objected.

The stranger handed him another gold piece. "Then that ought to just about pay your way there." His eyes suggested that Max do as he was told if he wanted to live until morning.

Fortunately, Max had the good sense this time not to push his luck. He took the gambler's money and moved over to Andy's Faro table.

The stranger settled onto the vacated chair and pushed his hat to the back of his head, openly raking Brett with eyes of approval. "Deal me in, honey. The name's Blade Palmer."

Brett wondered if that was supposed to mean something to her. It didn't. But, like Max, she knew trouble when she saw it so she covered her apprehension and her immediate dislike for Palmer with a cool smile. "As soon as this game is completed, sir, then I'll deal you in."

She returned to the game and finished it. To her dismay, the five men who had been at her table took the opportunity to collect their money, give their polite thank-yous and move on to other opportunities. It left Brett alone with the gambler.

He seemed to like that fine. "I guess it's just you and me, honey."

Brett's temper was rising. He'd chased off a good amount of profits and she didn't appreciate it.

While the thoughts roiled through her mind, her hands kept moving. She split the two-pack deck and started shuffling. "Place your bet, sir. We have no maximum limit. The minimum is a dollar."

With elbows on the table he leaned as close to her as the table would allow. "I'm not interested in your deck of cards, sweetheart."

She didn't bat a curled lash. "Then perhaps you'd like a drink at the bar."

He smiled lasciviously. "A drink would be nice. But only if you'll share a bottle with me upstairs."

Brett sensed the latent danger ready to spring out of him. She held her cool. "The women here only deal cards, sir."

His smile slipped. Anger burned in the center of his black, alcohol-soaked eyes. He left his chair and came around to her side of the table and took her elbow, pulling her out of her chair and to her feet. The liquor on his breath nearly knocked her over. "No two-bit whore has ever refused Blade Palmer."

Brett's experience with wrangling wild mustangs had enhanced her intuition to know when it was time to let go of a rope or take a dally. With this renegade, it was time to do the latter. She looked him square in the eye. "Let me go, you

154

sorry son of a jackass, or you'll live to regret you ever walked into this establishment."

His upper lip curled in amusement. "And what exactly do you plan to do to make me regret it?"

By now the room had hushed; all activity had ceased. In the silence, Brett's voice easily cleared the room from one end to the other. "I don't like repeating myself, mister, but because you're obviously a little slow-witted, I'll explain it to you again. *The women at* The House of Cards *only deal cards.* Now, unhand me and get out while you can still do so on your own two feet."

To Brett's relief, Sam appeared with his six-shooter in hand. He butted the muzzle of it up against the back of Blade Palmer's head. "You heard my sister, pal."

Palmer's nostrils flared; rage filled his eyes. Brett was possibly the only one who saw the exact moment Palmer snapped. Letting out a roar, he whirled and threw himself full force into Sam, knocking him backwards onto the card table and crashing down on top of him. The table collapsed beneath them, busting into pieces.

Sam came up, rolling Palmer to the side, but he lost the revolver and it skidded across the room. Shouts broke out as a fist fight ensued. A few men tried to help Sam, but in a matter of seconds the entire place turned into a melee of fighting men. Cards scattered, all four tables were smashed. Chairs and liquor bottles were broken over heads. Brett and her sisters found refuge behind the bar, covering their heads with their hands as whiskey bottles flew over them, showering them with liquor and glass.

Brett spotted Sam's rifle on the shelf below the bar and reached for it. "I think those boys have had about enough fun for one night."

"Don't kill anyone," Andy eyed her fearfully.

"If I do, it'll only be that damn-blasted gambler who thinks he's such a ladies' man. Callin' me a whore . . . I'll show him."

Brett stood up and pointed the Henry skyward. "I hate to put a hole in the ceiling, girls, but maybe we can get Sam to fix it later."

CHAPTER FIFTEEN

A FOOT IN THE STIRRUP

It seems that when you're trying to keep a low profile, you always find yourself riding the rim. Well, that gun blast brought the sheriff and two deputies who looked like they had already reserved their seats in hell.

On the one hand, Delaney and her sisters were glad to see the law. On the other, they had the inclination to head right out the back door along with everybody else. Customers scattered, not wanting any association with the ruckus. Meanwhile, the girls were still hiding behind the bar, praying that the sheriff had never heard of the daughters of Luke McCall.

Sam finally got the best of Blade Palmer and hauled him to his feet by the coat collar—or what was left of it. He was just preparing to toss him out on his ear when the sheriff took charge of the situation.

"I see you finally got a tiger by the tail, Palmer. I was wondering how long it would be before you got your due." He handed Palmer over to one of his deputies who spun him around and put cuffs on him.

"Why are you arresting *me?*" Palmer snarled. "He's the one who started it."

Sam spoke up in his own defense. "When a lady says no, pal, she means no."

"She isn't no damned lady or she wouldn't be dealing

cards in a two-bit place like this. And she's going to regret this. That's a promise."

Delaney was about to come over the bar and give Palmer a sampling of the McCall temper. Luckily, she was spared the trouble. Sheriff Bailey didn't much like the man's mouth either.

"Haul him over to the jail," Bailey said to his deputies. "And the rest of you gawkers, clear out. The action here is over. There'll be no more tomfoolery tonight."

After the last of the customers had vacated the premises, the sheriff headed for the bar, stepping over broken tables, scattered cards, and a lot of money.

"Opening night?" He aimed the question at Brett. After all, the woman totin' the rifle is usually the person in charge.

"Yes, sir," Brett said. "And that yahoo mistook me for a sportin' woman. I had to set him straight."

The sheriff, not a bad-looking sort himself, perused her with an appreciative eye. "I'm glad you did, ma'am. Blade Palmer has needed it from the moment he came into town a couple of weeks ago. It's unfortunate he tore things up though. I'll see that he pays damages."

"We'd be obliged, sheriff."

"Name's Mark Bailey, ma'am."

"Pleased to meet you, Sheriff Bailey." Brett set aside the rifle and offered her hand.

When Bailey released it—after holding onto it a bit longer than Delaney felt was necessary—his gaze traveled over the rest of them lined up behind the bar on either side of Brett. They shook hands with him, and while they did he took in their every detail. In the business he was in, Delaney figured he had probably been trained not to forget a face. She was hoping he'd forget theirs, but that was wishful thinking. Men didn't forget pretty women, and right off he

158

commented on the twins being twins.

"Yes, sir. We are," Brett replied.

"It's always fascinated me," he said, gazing at them as if truly enchanted.

"What's that, sir?"

"Twins. The idea of two identical people."

"We just look alike," Andy offered. "We're actually as different as night and day."

He turned to Brett to get the other side of the story. "Is that so?"

"Yes, sir. It is."

Then he wanted to know their names. Brett told him the aliases they were using. He said, "I heard about the Taylor family. I figured I'd get over here sooner or later. I like to get to know all the new business owners in town. Too bad it couldn't have been under better circumstances."

Finally he pushed away from the bar, saying he needed to get back to work. "Things might have gotten off on the wrong foot for you, but I'm sure it'll smooth out now." He touched his hat in deference. "It's been a pleasure, ladies. Sam."

A week later Sheriff Bailey invited the twins to the theater and dinner. They accepted. After all, it wasn't a good idea to get on the bad side of the law.

The twins' relationship with Sheriff Bailey turned out to be quite advantageous. On their way past the jail, they stopped in to give him their well wishes, and it allowed them to keep an eye on the Wanted posters he had tacked on his board. They didn't know how deep his feelings for them went, but they did know he enjoyed appearing around town with one of them on each arm. They drew a lot of attention, and Sheriff Bailey basked in it. He treated them like queens and bought them gifts. Since everybody knew they were the sheriff's "girls," nobody bothered them.

By December, Truckee Pass was closed off by snow. The McCalls relaxed. Except for a few travelers making their way from California through the southerly Walker Pass or up from Arizona Territory, the only person traversing the snowy Sierras was the hardy mailman, "Snowshoe" Thompson, a Norwegian who used skis to make his way over the Sierras to Genoa and back with the mail bags. It was unlikely that any bounty hunters would find their way to Virginia City before spring, but those Wanted posters still might crop up in Sheriff Bailey's mail.

At *The House of Cards*, the "Taylors" had a full house every night. Word had spread among the men that the girls only dealt cards, and if there was ever a miner who doubted it, Sam was quick to make sure they understood. He was good at assuming a rattlesnake look, so customers tended to stay out of his striking range.

While the twins let Sheriff Bailey escort them on their days off, Hank and Delaney—the latter having turned twenty a week before—found other things to do on their day off. There were chores and errands to be done so *The House of Cards* could run smoothly the rest of the week. They also exercised the horses.

Sam spent a portion of each day waffling between duty and desire as he lived one life and kept the other secret. At times, he practically forgot why he'd come to Virginia City. His position as hunter had turned to protector, and he'd settled into the role as bartender and brother.

He didn't know why he was waffling. He'd always done the job he set out to do and moved onto the next one. He'd come to take advantage of a woman who had drawn the lust from him, and he hadn't expected that feeling to change. Daily contact with the McCalls had almost convinced him of Stark's perfidy.

On the Sunday before Christmas, he strapped on his .44, figuring to do some target practice. Someone lurking in the shadows outside the card house the night before had caused him some concern.

He didn't rule out another bounty hunter showing up either. Stark had said he'd release the Wanted posters in two months if Sam hadn't captured the McCalls by then, but Stark was a liar.

He didn't know exactly what he was going to do about the girls, but he *did* know he didn't want them killed. He'd invested too much time in them to let someone else walk away with the bounty. But it was more than the money. He had seen plenty of bounty hunters in the past few years. They were in the business for money. Some were no better than the outlaws they hunted. Some were worse.

He worried about Sheriff Bailey. He didn't like the man's relationship with the twins. Stark had failed to mention on the Wanted poster that two of the McCalls were twins. If Stark corrected that oversight, and sent out more posters— and if Sheriff Bailey got his hands on one of them—he'd have the sisters locked up faster than a Deacon taking up a collection. Damn, why didn't he just get on with it? Arrest them and take them back over the mountains to Hawk's Point and collect the money. Was he stalling because it was winter? Or because he knew they were not real criminals?

He slid the revolver into his holster, then removed the photograph from his saddlebags. He sat down on the edge of the bed and stared at it. Confusion and a turmoil of emotions clouded his judgment. His eyes lingered on Delaney. What had he hoped for anyway by infiltrating her life? A full confession? Did he want her to trust him enough to tell him everything, to turn to him for protection from Stark? But where did he want to go from there? Did he want her? Would she want him? Would he betray her and her sisters in the end? It would have all been so much easier if his conscience and his heart had stayed out of the way.

A knock at the door startled him. He shoved the photograph under his pillow. With thoughts of Palmer and Stark fresh in his mind, he drew his six-shooter again. "Who is it?"

"Me. Delaney."

The sound of her voice sent a tingle of excitement down his spine. Why was she coming to his room? He felt the rise of desire every time he looked at her from across the gaming room, or even when her image appeared in his mind.

He went to the door and opened it, forgetting he still held his revolver. She looked agitated.

"Is something wrong, Laney?"

She glanced at the gun. "I might ask you the same question."

"I was going out to target practice."

She breezed past him into the room and started pacing around, going to the window, then inspecting the Henry he'd left on the table after having cleaned it earlier. He positioned himself between her and the pillow.

"Not only are the twins gone," she said, "but Hank went to the theater today with some miner. I'm about to go cabin crazy. Do you want to go for a ride? You could still target practice and I could watch. I need to get out of this place."

"It's cold."

"You've got a tough hide."

He smiled. "I didn't mean it in the sense that it would bother me. I was concerned about you."

"It was you who caught the cold in the Sierras that nearly turned to pneumonia."

He chuckled. "True. But then, if you ladies had shared your bed with me and kept me warm," he gibed, "maybe I would have fared better."

She clicked her tongue in mild disgust. "I always knew you weren't a saint."

"I never claimed to be."

"Hank and the twins think you walk on water."

"But you know better."

"I certainly do."

"You get at least six proposals for marriage every day, Delaney. And I'm chasing a minimum of a dozen men away from you every night. Yet you don't let any of them court you the way your sisters do."

She wasn't offended or troubled in the least by his observation. "Unlike my sisters, I have a low threshold for bullshit."

"Not all men are full of it."

"And I suppose you don't think you are?"

She perused him in a way that made him warm all over. "No, but you probably wouldn't agree with me."

"You're right. I don't agree with you on anything."

He rechecked his load, purely out of habit, before sliding his six-shooter back into the holster on his hip.

Delaney eyed the action. "You handle that weapon like a man who is very familiar with it, Sam. Are you sure you're not an outlaw? Or a lawman?"

He met her probing eyes. She was leading him right into a trap. Did she know who he was? Did she suspect? What would she do if he suddenly told her the truth? That he'd followed her and her sisters for bounty then fallen hopelessly in love with her.

"Not the last time I looked." He gave her another disarming smile and settled his hat more firmly over his dark hair. "I'll go riding with you. What do you say we see if we can find some mustangs out there on the desert?"

He'd hoped her eyes would light up like stars, instead he saw wariness there.

"We'll take some blankets and a picnic lunch," he added.

She laughed. "A picnic in December? This isn't southern California."

He shrugged. "There's not much snow out on the desert. We could find a spot to spread the blankets. The worst that could happen is that it might snow. It's better than sitting around here playing solitaire."

She laughed. "If I have to look at a deck of cards today, you might be searching for a straight jacket and a madhouse."

"Then let's do it." He took her by the arm and ushered her out of the room and away from the pillow that hid the photograph. "I'll saddle the horses. You fix the lunch."

Sam slid his Henry into the saddle scabbard and took in the town with a practiced sweep of his eyes. The stranger he'd seen last night was out there somewhere. Was he one of Stark's men? If he was, he might be after Hank and the twins right now. Sam hadn't liked them leaving this morning, but he had nothing solid to base his feelings on.

There was also the question of where Stark was. Obsessed with the McCalls' capture, he could have figured out by now where they'd gone. He could be here, having come in by way of Walker Pass. It was already evident that Stark didn't trust Sam to get the job done. How many others had the cheat hired? And how many would he kill when he had what he wanted?

Sam led the horses down the street and up the hill to *The House of Cards*. It would warm them up before he and Delaney got in the saddles. He'd put Delaney's sidesaddle on, knowing that was how she'd been riding since she'd arrived in Virginia City. Knowing, too, how she hated it. He'd heard her to saying to Hank one night, "This card house is fine and dandy, sis, and we've had fun and made more money than we ever did mustanging, but this isn't home. This isn't us. I want Daddy back and our little *cabaña*. I'm tired of being indoors with smoke burning my eyes and strange, ugly men making passes. I just want to be free again, riding over those hills after mustangs, hell-bent for joy."

That confession had touched Sam in a way nothing else had. Not just for Delaney and her sisters, but for himself as well. He was a Harvard-educated man, come West to practice law. But he had soon wearied of defending men who needed to hang. It was then he'd put on a gun, learned how to shoot it, and found that it fit naturally in his hand. It had carried a heavy burden of responsibility. Now, like Delaney McCall and her mustangs, he was having a terrible hankering to run free.

Delaney could have enjoyed her ride more if Sam hadn't been on edge. He kept looking around, as if expecting Indians to pop up over the top of every hill. He'd even brought his field glasses and put them to his eyes every few minutes. He said he was looking for mustangs, but his searching eyes were too vigilant.

He said, "I've heard there are as many mustangs over in this desert land as there are in the Great Valley."

They had never told him about their mustanging days, and Sam had never asked about their past. Nor had they asked about his for fear they would have to reciprocate. There were times when Delaney still toyed with the notion that, like them, he might be hiding from the law. So now she wondered if it was only coincidental that he had suggested they search for mustangs, almost as if she should be impressed with the possibility of seeing them. She was, but she had tried to hide her anticipation. Of course, mustanging was as popular a pastime here in Virginia City as it was in California.

He handed her the field glasses. "There,"—he pointed to the east with excitement in his voice—"about two miles away. I knew we'd find them."

With practiced ease, and a heart beginning to pump wildly, Delaney found the band of mares and their young stallion. They were small in the distance, nearly camouflaged against the sagebrush hill they were grazing on. If there hadn't been a covering of snow, they would have been almost invisible.

"Let's get closer."

"I was hoping you'd say that." Grinning, he put the field glasses back in his saddlebags.

He held back, letting her take the lead. She was about to lay out plans to capture them, then caught herself. There would be none of that today. Just getting close enough to have a run with them would be enough to satisfy her hungry heart.

She and Sam snuck up on them, staying downwind, keeping to the valleys, winding their way through the hills until they were within a half mile. Shortly, the stallion sensed the danger. He tossed his head up, sniffed the wind, then spotted them on the knoll. He let out a squeal, giving the signal for flight.

"Let's race him!" Delaney leaned forward in the saddle. The buckskin knew what she wanted and broke into a gallop, leaping sagebrush, rocks, a dry creek bed. He was sure-footed and nimble and seldom stumbled, but Delaney wished she had her California saddle so she could lean out over the buckskin's neck and feel his black mane whipping in her face. But she held her seat expertly on the sidesaddle even though the buckskin pushed for his top speed.

She heard Sam's bay thundering up alongside. She flashed a smile at Sam before putting her concentration back on the ride, the terrain, and the wild bunch fleeing their pursuers.

Feeling an exhilaration she had missed more than anything in the world, Delaney raced with the mustangs and with Sam until she knew it was time to pull the buckskin in. He hadn't had a run like that for months now; she didn't want to break his wind. He came to a prancing halt, against his will. Like her, he had missed running with the wild bunch.

She patted his neck and turned him around so he would know they weren't going to pursue the mustangs any longer. "Buck isn't used to not capturing them," she called out to Sam with a smile, realizing too late she'd dropped a clue to her past.

Sam didn't seem to notice, or maybe he hadn't heard. He pulled the bay up next to her and they put the horses into a walk back toward Virginia City. "You're an impressive figure on horseback, Laney. Did anybody ever tell you that?"

She was pleased as punch to get such a compliment from Sam. "No, I guess not. But you don't do too badly yourself. My father was always impressive—" She caught herself, hoping he would let it drop.

"I was never that close to my father," he offered. "He made saddles to order back in Tennessee, and had a lot of wealthy customers that were willing to pay top dollar. He literally worked his fingers to the bone. When he came in at night he was too tired and ornery to even talk and he would just fall asleep. I vowed I wouldn't be like that. I vowed I would enjoy the simple things in life. Then I found out a man has to make a living—" His smile slipped but he caught it, as if he was determined not to fall into the quagmire of life that hadn't met his youthful expectations.

She looked away, sensing something intimate bringing them together, closer than was safe.

She had admitted to no one but herself that her attraction to Sam had grown considerably over the past two months. But regardless of how her heart felt about him, she was occasionally reminded to be suspicious, like earlier when he had handled that gun like a bona fide gunslinger. Still, if he'd meant them harm—if he'd actually been a bounty hunter—then he would have moved on it a long time ago. No, he'd been nothing but a genuine friend to them.

She turned away from his handsome visage and allowed her gaze to absorb the beauty of the austere Nevada hills. She found she could fall in love with the vastness and freedom on this side of the mountains as easily as she had the other. There was something about wide, open spaces that found its way into her soul and touched something there that nothing else in the world could touch. As long as she could have that freedom, then maybe it wouldn't matter where she was. At least it was some consolation if she should never get back home.

"That looks like a good place to have our picnic," Sam said, pointing to a little valley warmed by the sun and protected from the breeze. It received the southern sun and most of the snow had melted.

They rode into it and he quickly put together a fire made of sagebrush. Delaney spread the blankets nearby and the food. She'd brought fried chicken, hard-boiled eggs, rolls, fresh honey butter, ice-cold water, sweet pickles, and chocolate cake. They ate in silence, enjoying the warm winter sun on their backs, the joy of being away from town, and being together.

"It's beautiful," she said. "I didn't think so when we first laid eyes on it, but it grows on you."

168

"Do you miss home?"

She looked toward the Sierras, a high wall to the west that seemed so completely insurmountable. Yet they had crossed it in a foot of snow. The hardships of that journey came back sharply at times as did the loss of the man they'd left on the other side.

"Yes, I miss it. I wanted to hold onto that idyllic life we had forever with all of us together. Now, I see it slipping away, like running mustangs, right before my eyes. Sometimes I feel as if things will never be the same again."

"You could always go back."

She shook her head sadly and watched her words carefully. "If I did, I'm afraid I'd have to go alone. My sisters have been talking about their dreams for the future, dreams that will take us all in separate directions. It doesn't seem to bother them. They apparently don't miss the life we had bad enough to want to go back to it. They don't feel the need for us to stay together as a family. Brett tells me I'll just have to live with the change. That sooner or later we all have to live our own lives."

"A person does have his or her own life to live, Laney. Siblings can't stay joined at the hip forever. Most don't want to. I think it says a lot for your family, and for you, that you want them to remain a part of your life."

Delaney suddenly looked at Sam as if she was seeing him for the first time. Could she possibly trust him with her secrets? Who was he? Really.

He shifted uneasily under her scrutiny, then flashed a dubious smile. "What? Do I have egg on my face?" He reached up and wiped his lip, just in case.

She chuckled, then fell into seriousness again. "You don't know all there is to know about my sisters and me."

A veil fell over his eyes. Slowly he reached out and placed a finger to her lips. "I know all I need to."

He leaned toward her, close enough that she could feel his body heat. His hand, gentle but rough textured, slipped down along her neck, along her shoulder.

"You can tell me everything some day, Delaney, but not today."

Tenderly his lips touched hers, creating a warm, glowing sensation. She had barely had a taste of him, barely moved to respond, when a gunshot blasted the stillness, flinging him forward into her arms.

CHAPTER SIXTEEN

IN A LATHER

His blood covered her dress front. "Sam! Oh, my God!"

Another bullet landed in the ground by her knee. She set him away from her, yanking his revolver from its holster. Rolling away from him to draw the assailant's fire, she came up shooting, but all she saw was a man running away from a distant knoll. With fear in her heart, she lowered the revolver and turned to Sam.

He was trying to get up. Gently, she pressed him back down. "Don't move, Sam. You're hurt bad."

He covered the bloody wound with his hand. "I'll be all right."

Delaney wondered if the bullet had been intended for her. Had the gunman been one of Stark's bloodhounds—or Stark himself? If it *was* her he'd been trying to kill, he'd be back. "Can you ride, Sam?"

He nodded and she helped him to a sitting position. The color had drained from his face and pain was settling into his eyes. He might think he was going to make it, but she wasn't so sure.

"Let me get you bandaged up," she said.

Obediently, he waited while she shook crumbs off the linen napkins, refolded them to the clean side then tore the lace flounce off her petticoat to tie them in place over his wound. She placed his left arm close to his chest and immobilized it with the flounce.

"Okay. That'll have to do. Let's get you on your horse."

He was able to hoist himself into the saddle. Delaney handed him the reins then swung onto her buckskin. Moving out, she scanned the horizon and saw no sign of the bushwhacker.

"Who've you got after you, Sam?"

"I'm not wanted by the law, Laney. At least, not as a criminal."

"What's that supposed to mean?"

"Just get me to town. I'll tell you about it later."

Sam had weakened considerably by the time they reached the doctor's office an hour later. Blood soaked the makeshift bandage. With the doctor's help, they got him inside and on the table.

There was no bullet to remove. It had gone in through his back and come out through his upper chest below his collarbone. "He's a lucky man," the doctor said, stitching the wound up the best he could. "If he makes it through the infection that's bound to follow, he should be good as new."

As Delaney sat by Sam's side, waiting for him to wake up from the chloroform, she found it unsettling to realize that, on its exit, the bullet had barely missed finding its mark in her.

Several hours later, with Delaney's assistance, Sam stretched out on his bed at *The House of Cards* and allowed her to pull off his boots and cover him with a quilt.

"I'll fix you something to eat," she said, turning from the bed. He caught her hand.

"Wait."

"What is it, Sam? Do you need something? Water maybe?"

"No." His eyes probed hers deeply, as if he was trying to

see all the way to her soul. "I just need you . . . to stay with me."

Before she could respond, his eyes closed and he fell into a laudanum-induced sleep. She reluctantly released his hand and covered him to the chin with the blanket. Leaving the room, she wondered if the look in his eyes could possibly have been love.

The wound festered and turned ugly, just as the doctor had warned. Fever set in. Guilt-ridden, Delaney feared that the bullet Sam had taken might have been meant for her. She agonized over whether she should tell him the truth. In the end, she said nothing.

She spent less time at the card tables so she could take care of him. As the fever worsened, she had a hard time keeping him in bed. Half out of his mind, he appeared behind the bar to fix drinks. She and Andy persuaded him back to bed.

"I wish I had Juan Castillo nearby," Delaney said with a knitted brow the following Sunday. She and Andy were slicing up homemade noodles to drop into some chicken soup. "That old *curandero* would know what plants to put on Sam's wound to draw that poison out."

"I hear there's a woman over on Tam Street who grows all kinds of herbs in her backyard," Andy said. "She might know of something that would work."

It was agreed that Andy would go and Delaney would finish the soup.

While the noodles cooked, Delaney went upstairs and bundled up the laundry so it could be dropped off at the Chinese laundry. Brett and Hank were at the theater again. Hank had gone with a young miner named Denny Wilde. Sheriff Bailey's interest had leaned toward Brett, so Andy had gracefully stepped out of the triangle.

"She's better suited to him," Andy had explained to Delaney once the others were gone.

"Heck, Brett's not serious about him, Andy. She's just using him for a good time. As for Hank, I hate to see her spend too much time with Wilde. He tries to control her too much."

A wistful look had crossed Andy's soft features. "Bart Breckenridge is completely smitten with Hank, and I think she likes him, too. They'd be a better match. We need to make her see that."

"As long as we're wanted by the law, none of us will ever be able to lead a normal life. Maybe Hank knows we'll never be able to return to California."

A knowing look had entered Andy's eyes. "Speaking of marriage and such, is it my imagination, or are you and Sam sort of sweet on each other?"

Delaney's face had flushed and she'd plunged wholeheartedly into the meal preparation. "I like Sam. Who doesn't? He's about as handsome as they come. But he isn't good marriage material. He's a drifter. Maybe even an outlaw."

"Maybe he's drifting until he finds a reason to settle down. Like the right woman. It might even be you."

Putting the old conversation aside, Delaney dropped the bundle of laundry next to Sam's door. "He might be handsome," she grumbled, "but marriage is one bag of oats I'm not so sure I want around my neck."

She quietly opened his door and tiptoed closer to the bed, finding him asleep. She saw right away the red flush and beads of perspiration showing through two days of black stubble. The doctor had warned her of this. She needed to get some ice water and get the fever down.

She was about to turn from the room when she saw something that looked like a photograph tucked carelessly into his saddlebags next to the bed. She knew she should mind her own business, but curiosity got the best of her.

Slowly she withdrew the photograph. One look sent her stumbling backward. She bumped into the chair and sent it scraping across the hardwood floor with a yowl.

"Delaney," came Sam's weak voice. "It's not what you think." He tried to rise from bed, to reach for the photograph.

She backed toward the door, gripping it tightly in her hand.

"Who are you? Why do you have this! You're one of them, aren't you?"

He got out of bed and came toward her, half-naked and with fever-glazed eyes. She bumped up against the door. He leaned into it with both hands, either using it for support, or making sure she didn't escape.

"If I was one of them, why would they try to kill me?"

"We both know that bullet could have been meant for me."

"Stark hired me to find you," he conceded. "But things have changed, Delaney. I began to suspect that you and your sisters were innocent. I'm here now to protect you . . . from him."

"You deceived us!"

"Yes, I did. I had to. You helped me to change my mind about who I was and what I wanted in life—"

"Shut up. I don't want to hear your lies." She pushed at his chest that pressed much too close.

He staggered back, thrown off balance. "Delaney, let me explain—"

She yanked the door open and ran from the room, still clutching the photograph. He came after her.

She raced behind the bar and grabbed the Henry rifle, stopping him dead in his tracks. "Stay where you are. I don't want to shoot you, Sam, but I will. God, how could you trick us? When were you going to turn on us and haul us back to Stark? Have you already let him know where we are?"

"I wasn't going to tell him. But I was going to try to clear your name."

"You're a *bounty hunter!*" She made it sound as if he were slime in the bottom of a stagnant pond. "Get back in that room. I'm going to lock you up until we decide what to do."

"Delaney—"

"Don't Delaney me. Move!"

He returned to his bed where he collapsed, unable and unwilling to put up a fight. He stared at the ceiling as she locked the door and cursed him some more.

"We trusted you, Sam Saxton. Damn you. Damn you to hell!"

Delaney was pacing the floor like a broomtail trying to escape a blind corral when Brett and Hank burst through the door, laughing and talking about the theater show. One look at her and the smiles vanished from their faces.

"Delaney, what's wrong?" Hank asked.

She held up the photograph. "Sam. It was him. He took it. He's a damned bounty hunter, hired to take us in. I thought he liked me. He kissed me! The no-good bum was probably laughing at me the whole time."

"He *kissed* you? When?"

"The day we went riding. Oh, what difference does it make!"

"Where is he?"

"I locked him in his room."

Brett took the photograph. "We should have let him die— both times."

"What are we going to do with him now? He hasn't done anything against the law so we can't have him arrested."

"No, not without getting ourselves arrested too."

"This is going to force his hand. We'll probably have to leave Virginia City."

"Why didn't he arrest us before now?"

"He was probably just waiting for the snow to melt to haul us back to California, and using me in the meantime," Delaney replied bitterly.

They pondered their situation and finally worked themselves into rationalization.

"I think he's probably telling the truth," Hank said.

"He could have told us," Delaney snapped.

"There was a lot we didn't tell him either."

"And for good reason."

"Quit defending him, Hank!"

A child's voice from down in the saloon carried up the stairs. "Is anybody here? Hey, Taylor sisters, I have something I'm suppose to give to you!"

They left the room and went downstairs. A twelve-year-old boy stood next to the bar with a cloth bag in one hand and a folded piece of paper in the other.

"What is it, young man?" Hank was the first to reach him.

He handed her the cloth bag. "That's some herbs from the witch lady over on Tam. This here's a note as to why your sister couldn't bring them herself."

"Did she give it to you?"

"No, some guy told me to deliver it."

When the note was safely in Hank's other hand, the boy ran back outside.

"What's going on?" Hank set the cloth bag on the bar.

"Andy was supposed to bring some herbs back for Sam's fever and infection," Delaney explained. "What's in the note?" She leaned over Hank's right shoulder; Brett leaned over the left.

Hank unfolded the paper and started to read aloud, but

the words froze on her tongue. A hand-printed scrawl leaped out at them:

I know who you are and I've got your sister.
If you want to see her alive again, come to the
Jim Dandy mine before midnight. Come alone.

CHAPTER SEVENTEEN

CROSS-HOBBLED

A drunken Blade Palmer shoved Andy into the mine. The lantern he held cast a dimly lit path for her to follow. "Sit down over there on that pallet," he commanded in a slur. "And start gettin' yourself out of those clothes. You're going to give me what you refused the first time. That ought to just about fill the space until your sisters get here."

Andy saw the pallet—some blankets spread over dried grass—and she stayed right where she was. He'd refused to tell her much of anything on the way here, only that he had been hired by Stark to track them down. Stark had figured out that they'd gone into Nevada, but he'd quit trailing them at Dutch Flat.

Palmer had taken over, mistaken her for Brett, and now intended on making her pay for that earlier altercation. After that, he would take them back to Hawk's Point to collect his reward money. Hank would suffer at Stark's hands before they were all hung. Sometimes it really was hell being a woman.

"I hate to be the bearer of bad news, Mr. Palmer, but you've got the wrong twin. Your victory over me is going to be hollow at best."

He jerked her around and held the lantern up higher, peering into her face. "You're lyin'."

"No, I'm Andrea. Or Andy, as my sisters call me. The twin

that refused your attentions was Brittany. She's a bit of a hot-head. Doesn't take too kindly to aggressive men. She likes to be the one in control. You'll really accomplish nothing by hurting me."

He thought about that, then a clever idea crowded into his liquored mind. "It'll hurt her worse knowing she was the cause of your demise. Now get over there and get your clothes off." He gave her another shove that nearly sent her sprawling.

She righted herself against the cold mine wall and pulled her cloak tighter.

Seeing she still wasn't going to obey, he pointed his gun at her. "I can shoot you without regret."

"None of this is necessary, Mr. Palmer. I could just *give* you what you want. I'm not like my sister at all." She was playing with fire, but maybe he was the sort who lost interest in the willing ones.

"Now, why would you do that?" he asked suspiciously.

"Because you're a handsome man. The kind of man a woman needs. However, I'd like it a lot better if I was warm. Could you build a fire in here?"

"I haven't got time to mess with a fire," he barked. "Besides, if you think you can get me to go lenient on you by seducing me, you've got another thing coming."

This wasn't going the way she'd hoped. "Why don't you look at this another way, Mr. Palmer—*Blade*. We might as well enjoy our liaison before my sisters arrive." She managed a seductive smile, but her heart was thudding so hard she sounded breathless. Maybe he would think it was passion. "Chances are they'll be a long while getting here."

"How do you figure?"

"You obviously don't know how long it takes a woman to get unbuttoned and out of her corset and stockings. Just unbuttoning one's shoes is a tremendously tedious affair."

"Why's all that necessary?"

"They can't ride out here in their good gowns, Mr. Palmer. They must wear proper attire."

"Quit stalling with this nonsense or I'll just shoot you."

Her brow furrowed. "Do you really want to haul a dead body all the way back to Hawk's Point?"

"Who said anything about hauling your body back? I'll just scalp you, or cut off a finger or something. Take an item of clothing."

"You don't know Eli Stark very well, do you? But then I guess you wouldn't, having just met him. He might be a lawman, Blade, but he's anything but honest or trustworthy. Why that no-good won't pay you a dime of that money he promised you if you don't have adequate proof. You could kill any blonde-haired woman, cut off anybody's finger—it wouldn't be proof enough for Eli. He'll probably set up a meeting with you out of town somewhere, under the pretense of paying you, then he'll shoot you between the eyes and leave you for the buzzards. If I were you, I'd get the drop on him before he got it on me."

Palmer waved his gun at her. "Get them togs off. I've decided I don't care if you're the wrong woman. You're every bit as annoying as the other one."

She could stall him no longer. She started to remove her coat when she felt the deck of cards in the pocket. A new idea sprang to mind.

"Could I have some of your whiskey, Mr. Palmer? If you won't build a fire, then maybe some Red Eye would keep me warm. We could have a few drinks, play a little card game or two." She gave him that warm smile again. "Like I said, Brett and I are nothing alike. You might have had better luck from the beginning if you'd come to me. I've always had a secret hankering to be a sporting woman," she lied, "and this little game is one that some of those ladies of the night play with their customers—or so I've heard."

"What have you got up your sleeve?"

"No aces, I can assure you. Actually I was thinking that we've got a considerable length of time to kill before my sisters get here. The way this game works is that we deal a hand of poker then whoever loses has to remove an item of clothing."

"What's the point if there's no money involved?"

"Why, Blade. When all of my clothing is gone, then, well . . . we'll do what you want. Any*thing* you want. In the meantime, the anticipation is so delicious."

He licked his lips.

"You're a gambler," she continued. "A lover at heart. Force isn't the style of a sophisticated man such as yourself. You don't have to do that to get a woman."

He straightened his shoulders, made himself an inch or two taller. "You're right. I don't."

"Then can you build a fire?"

His eyes undressed her. "I reckon."

"And the whiskey?"

"It's right there in my pack. I'll get it."

The Jim Dandy mine was over the hill toward Gold Hill. It had played out pretty quick and was abandoned. It was also stuck out in the toolies all by itself. Delaney, Hank, and Brett knew they couldn't hope for any help from anybody. By the time they got there, the sun had set and dusk was snatching the color from the land.

They paused at the base of the rocky hill and stared up at the mine's gaping mouth. A small campfire burned just inside. "How are we ever going to get Andy and ourselves out of this one?" Hank asked hopelessly.

Brett's outlook was no more optimistic. "He's got us all right. We can't go anywhere but straight into his trap."

Delaney touched the reassuring pressure of the hide-out gun in her boot. Their .44s were hidden in their bedrolls. "Maybe we'll be able to get the drop on him."

Hank's lips compressed into a hard line. Her back stiffened like a warrior preparing to step into battle. "Stark wants me. I'll strike a bargain."

"No you won't," Brett responded. "We won't sacrifice your life for ours."

Suddenly a voice called out from above. In the dim light they saw a man standing in the mine's entrance, holding Andy in front of him with a gun to her head. He was too small to be Stark.

"Come on up, girls." His voice echoed in the twilight. "And make it snappy or I kill her."

"I guess that answers our questions." Delaney took the slack from her reins and nudged her buckskin forward, leading the way up the hill to the mine.

At the top, they stopped three abreast and saw that the stranger was none other than Blade Palmer. He looked disheveled, as if he'd just gotten out of bed. All he was wearing was his trousers and a hip-length coat. He shifted from one bare foot to another. From the way he weaved unsteadily, and the way he slurred his words, they deduced he was drunk. They feared the worst, but Andy looked unruffled, almost . . . pleased.

"Oh, I remember you," Brett said smartly. "You said you'd get even with me. Well, let's settle this, mister. There's no need to drag my sisters into it."

He gave her a glassy-eyed glare. "I wasn't at your place to gamble the other night, or to whore. I was there to make certain the bunch of you were the McCalls."

"Congratulations." Hank crossed her forearms over her saddle horn. "We are indeed the McCalls, and if you've hurt our sister in any way, you're dead. Andy, are you all right?"

"I've been having a lovely time just watching my pal here tip the bottle," Andy assured them. "He was kind enough to play cards with me to while away the hours. Did you know he works for Eli Stark?"

"The sheriff seems to have a *lot* of men on his payroll," Delaney commented dryly.

"What do you mean?" Blade demanded.

"Just that you're not the only bounty hunter he hired to come after us. You might know the other one. He's the man you tried to kill a week ago. I assume that it *was* you who did the bushwhacking?"

"You're lying. If he was a bounty hunter, then what was he doing working for you?"

"Why did you shoot him if you didn't know who he was?"

"I was aiming for you," he said smartly.

That unsettled Delaney, but she kept a straight face.

"If he was a bounty hunter," Palmer continued, "he could have arrested you any time."

"He got sick coming over the Sierras," Brett put in calmly. "Maybe he was just waiting until he felt better. We're quite a handful when you get us all together."

"I don't believe you. Who is he?"

"He told us his name was Sam Saxton."

Fear streaked across Palmer's face. "*The* Sam Saxton?"

So, Saxton had some notoriety among the bounty hunter crowd?

"One and the same," Delaney said. "Of course we just found out ourselves about him being a bounty hunter. It was quite a shame."

"He'll pose no threat," Palmer insisted. "I might not have killed him, but he won't be riding for awhile."

"It takes a lot to keep Sam down," Delaney countered, "and I doubt he'll sit back and do nothing when he finds out you've muscled him out of his reward money. He's got a lot of time invested in us. He might even have you in his gun sights as we speak." Delaney knew it wasn't possible because she'd left him locked up in his room. How he would find a way out of there was anybody's guess. At the moment, she was still too hurt and angry to care whether he made it out or not.

But her bluff had the desired effect. Palmer glanced nervously into the encroaching darkness and swallowed down a lump so big it made his Adam's apple bob.

"So, Palmer, what's your plan?" Brett feigned boredom, as if this was all just an inconvenience. "Daylight's wastin'. Practically gone, as a matter of fact. You're going to have to make a move here real quick or go light some candles."

The sisters could smell Palmer's whiskey breath from four feet away and knew they'd better not push him too far. Their only hope would be if he passed out.

"Get down from your horses," he ordered. "And don't try anything that'll get your sister killed. We'll head out at daybreak. Lucky for you, Stark wants you alive. He plans to watch you hang."

"Stark lets you risk your neck, put up with the inconveniences and hundreds of miles on horseback, and he gets the glory." Hank gave that idea thoughtful consideration. "That sounds like Eli."

"How much *is* he paying you?" Brett peered at Palmer in the gathering darkness. For someone who liked strolling with parasols in fancy dresses and fluttering her eyelashes at rich, handsome men, she could look mean as the devil on Sunday when she wanted to.

"Stark's paying me a thousand dollars for the four of you."

Delaney settled back in her saddle, looking disappointed. "That isn't much to write home about, and it's going to be about the hardest money you've ever earned."

"You won't give me any trouble." He tried to sound confident. "I'll just shoot the bunch of you. You'll end up in a grave like your old man."

That brought the girls to attention.

"What *about* Daddy?" Delaney's brows shot together.

Palmer knew he'd hit a sore spot. "He's dead."

"How do you know?" she demanded.

"Because a grave marker and a lady doctor up in Dutch Flat say so."

"Were you there?"

"I was."

"I refuse to believe it." The others nodded in agreement.

"Suit yourselves. I saw the grave marker."

The girls were silent. The bottom fell out of Delaney's heart. She figured it was the same for her sisters, gauging by the stricken looks on their faces. She should have stayed with him. Shouldn't have been so worried about her own life.

"I'm going to kill Eli Stark."

"How you gonna do that locked up in jail?" Palmer goaded.

"We're innocent," Andy said. "Stark took the horses from us and didn't pay for them. Then he framed us and murdered a sheriff down in Monterey. Killed his own deputy too."

"That's hogwash," Palmer said. "You're trying to play on my sympathies so I'll let you go."

"We could give you twice what Stark's offering," Andy offered. "You don't want to see four innocent women hang, do you?"

"I make a living collecting bounty, not bribes."

Delaney sneered. "There's a difference?"

186

"I'm through with your games." He pressed the revolver's muzzle against Andy's head again.

Delaney feigned indifference. "Suit yourself, but I'd bet Stark's thousand, and a thousand more, that you'll be dead before we are. Like I said, Sam Saxton is probably already on your trail. He's been stalking that money a sight longer than you have. He won't accept you stepping in and yanking it out from under him."

"You're lying," he insisted. "That man isn't Sam Saxton. If he was, you wouldn't have gotten out of Monterey. Now, you all just get down off those horses and stand over here next to your sister so I can collect your weapons. I want the ones in your boots, too."

Losing every card game to Andy, and not getting what she'd promised, had left Blade Palmer in a raunchy mood. When the daughters of Luke McCall demanded to be fed something besides whiskey, and hadn't brought anything in their packs but underwear and hardtack, he became enraged.

"We didn't exactly pack for a picnic in the country," Brett remarked dryly. "Due to the urgent nature of your note, the only extras I managed to grab were my mirror and my tweezers. And I only remembered those because I don't go anywhere without them. If I did, my eyebrows would look like California chaparral in a week's time."

Palmer gave her a liquored stare. "I told you, there's whiskey in my pack."

"We just figured that since you were taking us prisoner," Hank added, "that you would supply the food."

"What *are* you going to do about the situation?" Delaney needled. "You can't expect us to ride all the way to Hawk's Point on empty stomachs."

"He's just going to have to go to Gold Hill and get some

supplies," Andy said, matter-of-factly. "Aren't you, Blade?"

He threw down his whiskey bottle. It hit a rock and broke. "All right, damn it. I'll go to Gold Hill if it'll shut you up. Christ Almighty, I don't know that I've ever heard so much squawking except what comes from a hen house."

He tied them up tight and took off for Gold Hill like a man with banshees on his tail. When he came back an hour later with a few measly items in his saddlebags, and a couple more bottles of whiskey, the sisters were not happy.

"That won't get us two days out," Delaney complained. "We can't live off whiskey. We might run a card house but we don't drink. It's not ladylike."

Palmer's face turned the color of a chili pepper. "I don't like my decisions or my intelligence questioned by a bunch of mouthy women in trousers. And, frankly, I don't give a damn if you're dead or alive when we ride into Hawk's Point just as long as I get my money."

"Lugging dead bodies across California seems like a pleasant enough pastime," Andy quipped. "It's not very conversational, but—"

"Oh, shut your mouths! All of you! We'll go through Mormon Station. I'll get some food there and it won't cost me a dime. Those Mormons are real generous."

He was right about the Mormons. They were more than generous and even offered for them to stay a while. However, on the first night, when the Elders came to their camp toting their Books of Mormon, preaching the gospel of Joseph Smith, and telling the McCalls that their sins would be forgiven if they converted to Mormonism, the true religion . . . well, the McCalls were on their horses at first light. They learned that saddling a horse while wearing handcuffs got considerably easier when there was good incentive.

Palmer decided he'd underestimated them and re-cuffed

them with their hands *behind* their backs.

By the time they reached Walker Pass, a miserable two weeks later, Palmer's whiskey supply was dangerously low and the food was gone again. With no more Mormon settlements in sight, it was going to be a long ride across California.

"Maybe you ought to go hunting," Delaney suggested. "See if you can kill a rabbit or maybe a nice, succulent pine hen. Hank can cook the best pine hen you'll ever taste. Why, just thinking of it makes my mouth water."

"And why would I want to do that and leave the bunch of you alone?"

"Where are we going to go?" Hank asked. "The nearest town is two weeks in any direction."

"There's still some hardtack and coffee," he countered.

"There's two biscuits, last count."

"I don't do well if I don't eat regularly," Andy said for the hundredth time. "I get so weak I can hardly sit upright in the saddle."

"I don't care if you bitches are all dead when I get to Hawk's Point. Just as long as I get my money."

Being called derogatory names didn't settle well with the McCalls. They'd been through about enough and Palmer wasn't the only one with a short fuse. Delaney's was the first to blow. "Listen, you mangy skunk, I thought you said Stark wanted us alive so he could see us hang. If you bring us in dead and deprive him of his sick satisfaction, he definitely won't think twice about shooting you. He's been known to kill people for a lot less."

"Your life is short anyway where he's concerned," Hank put in. "He'll never pay you that reward money."

Brett agreed. "If I were you, I'd get while the gettin's good."

Palmer leaped to his feet. "Christ Almighty! I can see why

the man wants to hang the whole bunch of you! I'd do it myself right here and now if I had a good length of rope."

"Then you wouldn't get your reward money," Brett reminded him.

"All right! I'll go see if I can find a damned rabbit to kill if that's what it's gonna take to shut you all up. But first, nature calls, so you'll just have to hold your horses a while longer."

He made them get down off their horses and sit shoulder to shoulder around a big tree. He tied their feet and made his way out into the bushes.

An hour later, he still hadn't come back.

CHAPTER EIGHTEEN

TIGHTENING THE CINCH

"This leaves us in a real fine pickle," Delaney complained. "Here we are hog-tied, handcuffed, without food, and in the middle of nowhere."

"And it's not exactly warm," Andy put in.

At first, the girls hadn't given much thought to the duration of Palmer's absence until ten minutes stretched into twenty, twenty stretched into thirty, and thirty into sixty. "Let's see if we can find an extra key to these handcuffs," Brett said. "Any fool would carry a spare."

"He's not just any fool," Hank remarked.

Delaney was already to her feet. The situation had her in ill humor, and the cold only served to compound her churlishness. She hopped to his packs and saddlebags. The others joined her for the search. Maneuvering around, they got their hands on the bags, got the buckles undone, and dumped everything out onto the ground.

No keys.

Andy had been keeping an eye out over her shoulder, just in case Palmer, or something equally as unpleasant, should appear. "He can't fault us for trying to get away," she said nervously. "What do you suppose happened to him anyway?"

Delaney followed Andy's gaze, thinking their good fortune of being shuck of a stupid bounty hunter was too good to be true. "Any number of things. He's so drunk he could have tumbled down the mountain, fallen off a cliff. He could have even gotten turned around. Or, who knows, maybe a bear ate him."

"Maybe Indians got him," Brett optioned.

That thought startled Hank. "If there *are* Indians in these mountains then we need to find a key to these handcuffs. Fast. Come on, he's got a couple more packs."

They scooted, slid, got up on their feet, and hopped around some more. After considerable sweat and strain, they emptied out the rest of his belongings.

No keys.

They did find a hunting knife and immediately positioned themselves so they could take turns sawing the ropes off each other's ankles. It didn't solve the problem of their hands cuffed behind their backs.

"If we could get our hands in front of us," Hank said, "we could at least saddle our horses and get out of here. Let's try slipping our arms under our fannies and pulling them up over our legs."

Before the words were even out of Hank's mouth, Delaney and the twins were already at work stretching and contorting. In no time, they had the feat accomplished.

"All right," Delaney proclaimed, beaming and leaping to her feet. "Let's get moving. We can cut straight across to the Salinas River Valley and head home. Nobody will think to look for us there, at least not for awhile. Then we can head for Juan Castillo's and have him saw these cuffs off."

"Ride all the way with our hands cuffed?" Andy clearly doubted the sanity in that.

"We've ridden this far," Hank said. "We'll manage."

"Then what?" Brett asked. "Bounty hunters will still be after us. What we need to do is get our name cleared—or board a ship that'll get us out of the country."

Suddenly Hank looked as if she might cry. "I'm so sorry for all this. If I'd just married Stark none of this would have happened."

Brett gripped Hank's hands in hers. "If you'd married him we'd have missed the adventure of our lives."

"Some adventure. What if Daddy really is dead? What if we don't get out of this alive?"

Brett meant every word she'd said. "It'll still be the adventure of our lives, won't it? Now, come on. We need to get moving."

They turned Palmer's horse loose, figuring it would follow them—which it did. There was still no sign of the bounty hunter when they headed down off Walker Pass as swiftly as prudence would allow.

Delaney found it difficult to turn her horse west. When they came out of the Greenhorn Mountains, following the Kern River, she felt the pull to head north to Dutch Flat and see their father's grave for herself. She knew she wouldn't be able to accept his death until she did.

She pulled the buckskin to a stop. Believing she might have seen something or sensed danger, her sisters reined up alongside her. "What is it, Delaney?" Hank asked.

"I can't believe he's gone," she replied quietly. "He was alive when I left him. . . ."

"None of us want to believe he's gone. When we get this mess straightened out, we'll ride to Dutch Flat. Maybe figure out a way to bring his body home and bury it on the ranch. Now, we have to keep moving."

Delaney swallowed hard. It was the best they could do for now.

She lagged behind the others. Once, she thought she saw a rider moving down a distant hill behind them. Then the sun passed behind a cloud and the ghostly image faded into the brush and the mountainside. She searched the hills again. Nothing. It must have been an illusion. It certainly couldn't have been Palmer since his horse was still with them.

Finally she gave the buckskin his head and loped to catch the others. It was a stupid thought, but she wondered if that ghostly image was their father, trying to catch up.

They took Cottonwood Pass and headed toward San Miguel. Delaney couldn't shake the feeling that the rider was still back there, although she didn't see him again until the morning she left camp and walked a short distance up the Salinas River to fill the canteens.

"Hold steady, Laney," came the all-too-familiar voice from behind her.

Lord, she would never forget that voice. It had always made the blood in her veins run like warm honey. She had to curb the urge to turn and throw herself into his arms. She had to remind herself just who he was and how he had deceived them.

She looked over her shoulder and saw him advancing through the dry grass, revolver steady in his outstretched hand.

"You look like hell, Sam. Should you really be out here? That gunshot wound was pretty bad when I left you."

"It's considerably better."

She returned to filling the canteens, refusing to act scared or to submit to him in any way. Besides, she wasn't afraid of him. She didn't believe he would kill her, but she could understand why he was mad at her.

"How did you get out of your room, Sam?"

"I don't think you really care."

She shrugged. "I guess I just figured somebody would

come along and rescue you sooner or later. Actually, I was hoping for later."

"I see you managed to get rid of Palmer. How did you accomplish that?"

Delaney lifted a brow in surprise. "With you showing up, I just assumed it was you who took care of him. If it wasn't, then how did you know he was the one who snared us?"

He looked bewildered. "I never saw him on the trail. But Bailey and I figured it had to be him. He disappeared from town the same time you did, and we knew he had it in for Brett. Then I found the note you left on the bed and followed you to the Jim Dandy."

Delaney wished they hadn't been so careless, but they'd been in such a hurry to get away. She stood up slowly and turned, canteen in hand, lifting her hands so he could see her cuffs. "He went off in the brush to take care of business and he never came back. Unfortunately, he had the key to the handcuffs with him."

"Well, now. That's convenient." He returned his Colt to its holster.

She didn't like that smug smile at all. "What do you mean?"

"Because I'm taking you and your sisters to Hawk's Point, Delaney. I've got a bounty to collect."

Sam Saxton might have been as big a double-crosser as Eli Stark, but he was a sight easier to look at, and he was definitely a better provider than Palmer. He got them all trussed to a big old tree and surveyed his handiwork with a satisfied smile.

"That ought to hold you until I get back from San Miguel with some provisions."

Delaney cursed him. Called him a no-good so and so. It

made him grin all the broader.

"Don't disappear the way Palmer did," Brett retorted. "At least he had the courtesy to leave us in a position where we could fend for ourselves."

Sam swung into the saddle. "I have to admit I'm impressed with the way the four of you survived the trip from Walker Pass wearing handcuffs. You must be some real crack shots when you've got both hands free."

They weren't about to tell him that they had spent quite a few hungry days in between managing to kill a rabbit or a quail. They definitely weren't about to tell him how much they were looking forward to him returning with some food.

"That'll be something you'll want to remember." Delaney gave him a deadly glare.

He leaned down from the saddle and brushed the back of his hand over her cheek. "Thanks for saving my life, Laney. Twice. Someday I'll repay you."

"With a noose around my neck?"

He reined away and lit for town on a lope. True to his word, he returned a couple of hours later and fixed them a meal of fried chicken and milk gravy, baking powder biscuits, real butter, and canned peaches.

When they were done, Saxton smiled derisively. "I hope you enjoyed that, ladies. You won't get anything near that good in jail."

They drew the attention of everyone at Hawk's Point as they straggled single file behind Sam on a lead line. They were more than humiliated to be seen in their dirty, wretched condition and handcuffed like common criminals. Delaney's face blazed with shame by the time Sam stopped his horse in front of the hoosegow. She figured the others felt the same, but Brett held her head as high as a prancing stallion. Andy faced her imprisonment stoically. Hank looked the most frightened, knowing she'd have to face Stark again.

Stark was kicked back in his slat-backed rocker, lounging on the jailhouse porch and reading the newspaper. Sam reined up in front of him. Stark didn't get his nose out of the paper until Sam said, "I've got your outlaws, marshal."

The chair hit the boardwalk with a thud and Stark was to his feet all in one motion, grinning like an Apache with a new knife. He hurried down the steps and out into the street, thumbs latched in his gun belt.

"I'll take my money now, Stark," Sam said.

"You're missing the father. The reward money was for all five."

"You know he died from that bullet of yours up at Dutch Flat. One of your other bounty hunters—a guy named Blade Palmer—said as much so don't try any of your conniving tactics on me."

Stark sauntered back to stand on the boardwalk. It made him a little taller as he faced Sam who was still horseback. "The price we agreed on was for all five McCalls, Saxton. I can't give you that much for only four of them."

Sam swung down from the saddle and looped his reins around the hitching rail. He stepped up on the boardwalk, face to face with Stark. He had that rattlesnake look in his eyes again.

"I'd have the father, too, if you hadn't interfered. I'm going to say this once and only once. You pay me the full price or I'll turn these women loose and you can go after them yourself. But let me warn you, they don't lead worth a damn."

Stark's brows shot together. He reached for his gun. Sam's cleared leather before Stark could get a good grip on his.

"You can't turn them loose," Stark objected.

"I can, and I will. I'll lock you up and leave you there until they're out of the country. Don't mess with me, pal. I've nearly died twice bringing this bunch in, and I'm in no mood for obstruction from you."

Stark looked the women over. It was clear what was running through his head. He wanted the McCalls decorating the gallows. And he wanted it done as quickly as possible. "All right. The money's in my safe."

The two of them headed inside. Delaney called out, "Don't turn your back on him, Stark. He'd double-cross the devil if he had a chance. He'll probably take that reward money then shoot you in the back."

Sam paused in the doorway long enough to shoot her a scorching glare before leaving them in the saddle to stare down the curious eyes of passersby and a few nosey kids who decided to taunt them.

Delaney had just about had her fill of being called "rope meat" and was swinging from the saddle when Sam and Stark showed their faces again. The children took off, squealing like pigs with the butcher after them. Sam was tucking something inside his pocket which she assumed must be his hard-earned reward money.

"Do me a favor, Saxton. Buy yourself a big steak with that money." She stepped past him then arrogantly shouldered past Stark. "Things are going to be a little tougher this time, marshal. We want privacy in this place and some hot baths and decent meals. You'll have to get a curtain in here, too, and some towels and new clothes."

"You'll get what I see fit to give you."

The marshal put them two to a cell and removed their cuffs. They collapsed onto the cots. To their surprise, Sam came in and leaned against the bars. "I think they have a valid point, Stark. You wouldn't want people to think you're abusing the prisoners. Besides, the daughters of Luke McCall are the finest ladies I've ever known."

"I thought you just said they hadn't been easy to deal with."

"True, but that doesn't mean they're not ladies, and I expect you to treat them as such. People around these parts like them, and they aren't going to cotton to them being in jail for crimes they didn't commit, let alone having you not taking good care of them."

"What do you mean? Crimes they didn't commit."

"Come on, Stark. You and I both know that you're the one who killed those people and didn't pay for the horses you bought from the McCalls."

"You'd be wise not to voice that opinion beyond this room."

"Is that a threat?"

"Make of it what you will."

Saxton shoved away from the bars. "I think I just did. And don't worry about your food and baths, girls. Marshal Stark here will make sure you get everything you need. As a matter of fact, he's heading out right now to get a tub and a drape to section off one of the cells for your privacy. Then he's going over to the restaurant and have them fix you up a big steak dinner. Ain't that right, marshal?"

Stark said nothing but his eyes filled Saxton with .44 slugs. Sam just returned the deadly look with an insolent smile. "Now, ladies"—he paused at the door and touched the brim of his hat in deference—"it's been my pleasure. I'll be back later to see that Marshal Stark is treating you in the manner to which you are accustomed."

Stark waited until Sam was gone before turning to Hank. "Too bad about your old man," he said, but there was no sympathy in his voice or in his eyes. "You could have avoided all this if you hadn't pulled that dirty trick on me, Henrietta. I told you you'd pay."

"I'll do what you want, Stark. Just tell me what it is."

The twins and Delaney started to object, but Hank held up her hand silencing them. Stark found it amusing that she was finally giving in.

"What would I want from you?"

"We both know what you've wanted all along."

He chuckled. "It sounds as if you're working up to a proposition, Henrietta."

"Let the rest of them go and I'll marry you."

"What makes you think I want to marry you?" he snickered. "What makes you think I ever did? But I do want to see you and your sisters hang for your crimes."

Hank gripped the bars. Her burning fuse finally reached the dynamite. "We've committed no crimes and you know it, you sneaky little bastard. Besides, the charges have been legally dropped. How are you going to get around that?"

"The horse stealing charge might have been dropped, but there's been several murders since then, including that of my deputy and the sheriff of Monterey."

"You killed them both."

"Maybe you and I know that, but nobody else does. Our crimes come back to haunt us, Henrietta. You double-crossed me, and for that you're going to hang. You and your family, one and all. My only regret is that your father isn't here to swing alongside you."

"Who will hang you for double-crossing us and the scores of other people in this county? And for all the underhanded dealings you've engaged in?"

"It's like I told *you* once before, Henrietta. I'm the power at Hawk's Point. Nobody can touch me. Maybe when that rope tightens around your neck, you'll finally realize that."

★ ★ ★ ★ ★

From her cot, Delaney stared up at the fly-specked, smoke-tarnished ceiling. She was beginning to feel right at home. "This is what you call full circle."

"Not completely," Andy replied. "Full circle would find us free and chasing mustangs again."

Brett propped her hands under her head. "I suppose this means I'll never get to Paris."

"I'm sorry," Hank said softly. "I knew I should have—"

"Don't even think it," Delaney cut her off. "We've always stood by each other, and we will to the bitter end."

"What I'd like to know," Andy said, "is what happened between Delaney and Sam that caused him to turn on us. The guy was obviously sweet on her."

All eyes shifted to Delaney. She left the cot and went to the window. "What makes you think anything was going on in the first place? He was biding his time until winter was over. Palmer forced him to move sooner, that's all." She rested her forehead against the cool, adobe wall. "I can't believe I was actually beginning to fall in love with him."

"I can't believe it either."

The bemused tone in Brett's voice drew Delaney's head around. "What's that supposed to mean?"

"If I recall, little sister, the last time we were in here, you were telling us all what fools we were to want to fall in love and get married."

Delaney returned to her cot and sat on the edge, putting her head in her hands. "I guess he just picked me for his guinea pig because he knew I was the most naive. I wonder if he'd tried to get more than a kiss if we'd had more time to work on it."

"Would you have *given* him more than a kiss?" Andy's brows came together.

Delaney stared at the floor. That was a tough question. She'd certainly felt like giving him more, and that had been a feeling she'd never encountered before in her life. It'd been a real nice feeling while it had lasted.

She leaned against the bars. "No, not without a preacher coming around first."

Silence lapsed between them as each fell into her own thoughts. Thoughts of lives gone, dreams shattered. They weren't even hungry when two waitresses from the restaurant across the street came in at supper time with four hot sirloin steaks, courtesy of Sam Saxton.

Delaney awoke the next morning to a young-sounding voice growing louder and louder, hollering something she couldn't discern. Irritated, she put her pillow over her head but the sound wouldn't go away. It grew closer until the words seemed right outside her window. Then she bolted upright.

"What the devil!"

All four of them were to the bars as the boy selling papers ran down the street, hollering, "Extra! Extra! Read all about it! The notorious McCall gang has been captured!"

Before the sun had reached its zenith, there was an angry mob outside the jailhouse. From the sound of things, they weren't in any mood to wait for a trial.

CHAPTER NINETEEN

CHOKING DOWN

When the mob gathered outside the jail, there was nobody guarding the McCalls except the new deputy, young Cecil Lawrence, and he looked so green Delaney figured his mama still had to mash his frijoles.

The mob shouted for Cecil to open the cell and release the prisoners. They told him if he wouldn't step aside they were going to bodily remove him.

Delaney found it real hard to believe that all the people at Hawk's Point who had known them and their father over the years would shift loyalties so fast and want to lynch them. The whole affair upset her something fierce. She went over to Hank's cot and held her hand.

"It's going to be all right, Delaney," Hank soothed. "Things will straighten out."

"Yeah, at the end of a rope." Delaney sat morosely for a minute, thinking it wasn't right that they should hang for something they didn't do.

"Wait a second!" Andy shot to her feet. "Listen. That mob doesn't want to lynch us. They're demanding we be released!"

They went to the cell windows. They couldn't see what was going on in front of the jail, but they could hear better.

"The McCalls aren't going anywhere!" Cecil hollered at the crowd in a voice more high-pitched than usual. "This matter will be settled at the trial! All of you, go home!"

"Did you read the newspaper, Cecil?" one man shouted. "That bounty hunter says Stark is the one who did the killing. He says Stark didn't pay the McCalls for those horses, and when they took them back, he accused them of stealing!"

Another man chimed in. "We've known all along what a crook Eli Stark is. He's blackmailed more people in this town than you can count. Had us so scared for our lives and our families' lives that nobody dared stand up to him! But this is about as far as he's gonna go! Saxton's right. We need to stand up for ourselves, once and for all. And for Luke McCall's daughters!"

Delaney looked at Hank. "What in tarnation did Sam do now?"

"It sounds like he told the truth, little sister." Brett was half-smiling. "I'll bet he had this figured all along."

"If he did, it was a low-down act on his part not to let us in on it."

Cecil was hollering from the boardwalk again. "I can arrest him now under suspicion of murder, but if you want him to pay for the things he's done to you, you need to come forward and let the law know so he can be legally charged and jailed."

A hush ran through the mob, then a murmuring, like bees humming, while the crowd deliberated whether or not to face Stark with personal complaints.

Then another male voice came loud and clear through the alley window. "You don't need to be afraid. If you help us put Stark behind bars, and then testify against him in a court of law, he's bound to hang."

"What's going on?" Delaney cocked her head to hear better. "That was Sam and he said 'if you help *us*.' "

"It sounds like he's working with Cecil."

"Yeah, using us as bait to get Stark hung. I don't know that I like being dangled over the cliff like that."

"Just as long as he doesn't drop us," Andy remarked.

"Yeah, or the line doesn't break," Brett added dryly.

After another ten minutes, Cecil and Sam subdued the angry mob and convinced them to go home. The girls' freedom was lost, at least for now. But the talk hadn't ended by a long shot, and, they hoped the action hadn't either.

"Hey, Saxton!" Delaney hollered. "Come in here! You've got some explaining to do!"

It was a moment before they heard Sam's boots crossing the hardwood floor in the outer office. He opened the door leading to the cells and stepped into the dimmer cubicle.

"I guess you heard all that," he said.

"Enough," Delaney said. "You're going to be worn out jumping back and forth across the fence. You'll probably have a few slivers to pull out too."

"I know which side I'm on."

"Do you? First you collect your reward money, then you use us as bait to get to Stark. Not that we don't appreciate your efforts on our behalf, but what if your plan backfires?"

"Then you'll have your day in court, Laney. I think the town sentiment is such that you'll have a fair trial now."

"You're the one who fired those people up. What have you been doing besides giving the newspapers interviews?"

"Visiting a lot of saloons and other establishments around town. My throat is hoarse, campaigning for your cause."

"Why didn't you tell us this is what you had planned when you caught up to us on the trail?"

"Because I didn't—and don't—know if it will work, and I didn't think you'd go along with it. Besides, I didn't figure you'd have much reason to believe me."

"You hit that nail on the head."

He settled on a bench that had been placed a few feet from the cells for visitors. "I figured you'd be safer in here than running loose," he explained. "I couldn't trust that Stark wouldn't have more bounty hunters out there waiting to shoot you all first and ask questions later. When I found out Stark had hired Blade Palmer, and maybe others, I knew he was only using me to find you. He never planned on paying me. Probably never planned on paying Palmer either."

He leaned forward and rested his elbows on his knees. Delaney decided he looked tired and figured he had a long way to go to be completely recuperated from his gunshot wound.

"Spending the rest of your life running isn't any way to live," he continued, as if he had to convince them of that. "You need to get this cleared up so you don't have to spend your life looking over your shoulder. For what it's worth, I believe in your innocence."

Delaney knew she should be grateful that he'd stuck around to help them and not just taken the money and run. But she wasn't ready to choke on words of gratitude, not after the way he'd deceived them in Virginia City. Getting into their family, for Pete's sake, pretending to be their brother, leading her on with pretty words and kisses and such. She felt like a bona fide fool for falling in love with him.

Hank joined Delaney at the bars and said the things she couldn't. "Thank you, Sam. We appreciate your efforts to help us. We understand why you did it this way. Now, I have a question for you. I think you were the one who warned us about Stark when we were in Sacramento. But why? You didn't even know us then."

"I was beginning to suspect that Stark had framed you. When he showed up in Sacramento, trying to undercut me, I figured he might be out to kill you. So I started following you

206

more as a bodyguard than a bounty hunter until I could learn the truth."

Delaney wasn't convinced he was, or ever had been, on their side. "Why not explain the situation to us? Or hadn't you decided whether to give up the reward money?"

"No, I hadn't decided," he replied honestly. "A man's got a living to make, and I wanted that money. I've been saving to buy land. I wanted Stark to hurt somewhere, if only in the pocketbook. The low-life owed me that much for double-crossing me."

Delaney wondered where Sam Saxton planned to settle. She knew she shouldn't give a hoot, but it would probably be far away from Monterey and the McCall ranch. "You're giving up bounty hunting for ranching? I find that hard to believe."

"It's time to get on with my life, Laney. Settle down, get married, raise a family."

Her tone was heavy with disdain. "I've heard that song one time too many. That's all my sisters can sing lately."

"There's nothing wrong with wanting love and security. When you're eighty years old and can't do anything but remember, don't you want grandchildren to tell your stories to?"

His comments seemed to be getting too personal. "I think you got sidetracked, Saxton," she said. "You were telling us why you lied to us."

"I didn't lie. I just didn't tell the whole story. I needed to know the truth about the four of you and your dad, and the only way was to get into your lives. I was hoping one of you would eventually confide in me."

"Daddy always said if you want to keep a secret, don't tell it to anybody."

"Your father was right, but it made my job a sight harder."

207

"All right, Sam. One last question. Did you think that because I was the youngest I might be the most gullible? That all you would have to do is lay on your charm and I'd tell you everything?"

Amusment glittered in his eyes. "A man can't win the pot, Laney, if he doesn't ante in."

He turned from the cell and started to leave.

"Watch your back, Sam. If Stark reads that newspaper, he'll come gunnin' for you."

Sam paused at the door, giving her a look that dove to the center of her heart and made it hurt like holy hell. "Thanks, Laney, but I imagine he already has."

Sam was right. Eli Stark had read the newspaper and figured out that he had fallen from grace in the eyes of the townspeople. He hadn't so much as shown his face in town since that article appeared. Nobody knew where he was, but everybody was sure he was hatching a plan to get even with the McCalls and to finish Sam off for his interference. Stark wasn't the sort to walk away from a battle until he could be the victor.

As for Cecil, he was on his own. He'd contacted the U.S. Marshal for some help in apprehending Stark. Then he'd deputized Sam, Bart Breckenridge, and a few other local men. He figured he needed someone to guard the McCalls at all times, so he traded off with Sam and Bart. Cecil had been taking the night shifts and sleeping on the cot in the outside office. Sam and Bart were taking the day and evening shifts. When they weren't on duty, they were riding with the locals, scouring the countryside for a clue to Stark's whereabouts.

Delaney and her sisters made the most of their helpless situation. They laid back in their cells, relaxed, played cards, had regular baths, plenty of food, and even got new clothes.

They worried. And they hired that San Francisco lawyer named Proffit just in case they ended up in court.

Everybody in town was clearly on their side. The newspaper wrote editorials in their favor. Mr. Potter came over to interview them and printed their side of the story. They kept expecting Eli Stark to show up in his own defense, but from all indications, he'd vanished off the face of the earth, just like Blade Palmer.

After everything the McCalls had been through, though, they should have learned not to get too comfortable. One night around two o'clock in the morning, in strutted Eli Stark, holding a gun to young Cecil Lawrence's head.

CHAPTER TWENTY

TAKIN' THE BIT

Stark pushed Cecil up to Hank and Delaney's cell. "Now, go in there and cuff those two." He shoved two sets of cuffs into Cecil's hand.

Poor Cecil didn't want to do it. He was shaking so bad he could barely get the key in the lock, but finally it clicked and Stark jerked the cell door open.

Cecil apologized when he put the cuffs on Hank. "I'm sorry, Miss Henrietta. Real sorry. This isn't my doing."

Stark seemed overly annoyed or distracted. He kept rubbing at the back of his neck as if he had a headache. He had no tolerance for Cecil's politeness. "Hurry up, damn it. Get the other one."

"What are you going to do with them?" Brett demanded from her cell.

Stark sneered. "Don't worry, missy. They aren't going anywhere without you and your look-alike."

Brett breathed an exaggerated sigh of relief. "You had me worried there for a minute, Eli. I'm certainly glad you're not going to leave me and Andy out. You'll have my gratitude right up to the day I kill you."

Stark's jaw clenched and unclenched. He looked like he might reach over and strangle Brett. Instead he rubbed the back of his neck again. "Put a gag in that one's mouth after you handcuff her, Cecil."

Stark stepped into the first cell far enough to grab Hank by the cuffs and yank her out. He pulled two more sets of cuffs out of his pockets and handed them to Cecil. Brett was hurriedly stuffing things into her saddlebags.

"You won't need those where you're going," Stark snapped as she threw the bags over her shoulder.

"I never go anywhere without my mirror and tweezers, Eli. Just exactly where are we going anyway?"

"To a tall tree where you're all going to swing."

"Damn, isn't he just the nicest man?" Brett said. "He's taking us out of this stuffy place so we can get some exercise. Good Lord, I don't think I've been in a swing since I was twelve years old." She willingly held out her hands so Cecil could put the cuffs on her. "Now, if he could just figure out a way to separate these bracelets. . . ."

Brett led the way from the cell, swinging those hips like she was already in Paris with a gaggle of men stumbling bug-eyed after her. She wasn't about to let Stark have the satisfaction of inciting fear.

Stark pushed Cecil back inside the cell and slammed the door behind him. "Don't you so much as make a peep, boy, or it'll be the last noise you'll ever make."

Stark hustled the girls through the door. Hank held back, digging her heels in. She struck him with a look so cutting it would have sliced a Redwood down the middle with one swipe. "This is between you and me, Eli. Leave my sisters out of it."

"They're already in it. They're going to die right along with you." He gave her a good shove this time and she stumbled, colliding with Delaney.

When Delaney had righted herself, she said, "You know, Stark, your ugly face is like a picture that's been hanging on the wall for about five years too long. I figure it's just about time to take it down."

"Wishful thinking, girlie. Wishful thinking."

"We'll see who's wishing before this is over," she stated boldly.

Stark gave her and Hank another shove toward their horses which were saddled and waiting in the alley. On his, they noticed a good length of rope, coiled and twisted into a perfect hangman's knot.

"You should be commended," Delaney said. "You must have stayed up all night fixing that knot."

"Get mounted," he ordered, "and don't try anything stupid because killing you now or later won't make much difference to me."

"I wouldn't fire that gun," Andy inserted as she hiked up her skirt so she could get her foot in the stirrup. "You might bring Sam and Bart down on us. I wouldn't want to catch a bullet meant for you."

Delaney was trying to get on the buckskin and having difficulty. "What a fine time to be caught in a dress and handcuffs both. We might as well be hamstrung."

"I can certainly oblige." Stark's eyes warned that he'd had enough of their wisecracks. But if he'd expected fainting women, he'd kidnapped the wrong bunch.

Brett was already in her saddle and pulling her skirt down over her knees. "You haven't got time for that, Eli."

"I thought I told Cecil to gag you."

She shrugged. "Maybe next time you'll be better organized."

Stark had the horses all tied together with a lead rope. He took a dally around his saddle horn. He headed down the alley on a slow, quiet walk, keeping his eyes peeled for anybody who might be up at this hour. He nudged the horses faster down the back streets. By the time they were out of the

Hawk's Point city limits, he had them in a lope.

They all knew they were riding to their deaths, but they weren't about to let Stark know how scared they were. Delaney's legs were even quivering so hard she could barely keep her feet in the stirrups. She tried not to focus on how she was going to die. She tried to focus on how she was going to escape. How she was going to kill Stark. Seeing him dead would be the only way they would live. For the life of her, though, no plan came to mind.

There was no chance to talk, so Delaney prayed that Sam and Bart and Cecil—and maybe a whole posse—would come after them. It depended on whether Cecil would dare raise a ruckus before dawn. Delaney had the sinking feeling that she and her sisters were going to have to get themselves out of this one.

Stark took the main road south to Salinas, figuring that their tracks would be lost in all the others. By a dry creek bed he left the road. At daybreak, he reined up in a stand of old oaks and looked them over with a discriminating eye. He took the opportunity to rub the back of his neck and to pick at something there that was clearly keeping him distracted.

Delaney leaned back in her saddle and eyed the oak trees. "You'll need a good stiff branch to hold the weight of four McCalls."

Stark looked up sharply from his picking. "You'll hang one at a time, starting with you."

Delaney glanced at Hank and the twins. The facade of flippant bravery was getting hard to maintain now that they were at their destination.

Stark rode to a fat branch and threw the rope over it. "All right, *Miss* Delaney. You're first."

He positioned her and her buckskin under the branch and

tightened the noose around her neck. He tugged on the free end of the rope until it fit tautly over the branch, then tied it off to the tree trunk.

Delaney's heart raced. She thought she might even faint. At least Old Buck stood stock-still, just as he'd been trained to do. For that, Delaney was grateful.

With the noose chafing at the delicate skin of her neck, she considered praying for a posse to come thundering into view, but decided that time might be better spent praying for her soul.

"Damn you, Stark," Hank spat. "What will it take to get you to call this off? Money? We've got thousands over in the Virginia City bank. We'll give it *all* to you if you'll release Delaney and the twins."

Stark walked behind Buck and checked the hanging rope again. He seemed to be enjoying himself.

"It's tight enough," Delaney assured him. "I don't think adjustments are necessary."

"Was your vendetta towards my dad and me worth giving up your life and country, Eli?" Hank demanded. If Delaney wasn't mistaken, she saw a murderous rage surface in Hank's eyes.

Whether Stark had or had not weighed the full ramifications of his actions, he didn't appreciate being forced to consider them now. "I'm the power at Hawk's Point. Those people are too afraid of me to say a word."

"Apparently you weren't in the shadows listening when the people of *your* town were ready to lynch you."

"They're all smoke and no fire."

"They'll come after you for this."

"It doesn't matter. It'll be too late to help you. You're going to watch your sisters hang, Henrietta. Then I figure you and I will spend a little honeymoon over at your daddy's ranch. From there we'll ride down to Los Angeles where no-body knows us. Maybe head over into Texas."

"You're leaving everything you've worked for all your life just so you can make me miserable? Make me pay? You really are a madman."

"I can come back here anytime," he snapped. "Besides, I was getting tired of being the marshal of Hawk's Point. There are bigger opportunities in Texas."

"Yeah, I've heard everything's bigger and better in Texas," Delaney commented dryly. "Probably even the hangin' trees."

Hank hammered away, hoping to somehow deter Stark. "Tell me one thing, Eli. Why do you want a woman who hates your guts and who intends on killing you the first time your back is turned?"

His smile had an evil twist. "There's gonna be satisfaction in breaking you down, Henrietta. All the way down, until you're groveling at my feet."

"And then?" The hatred deepened in her eyes.

"Then I'll give you over to a Mexican whorehouse. Let them finish you off. First, you're going to watch your sisters hang."

Tears pooled in Hank's eyes. She looked defeated. "I'm sorry, Delaney. God—"

Delaney's heart filled with love for her oldest sister. "It's all right, Hank," she said as bravely as she could. "We had some good times. We stuck together to the end, like family should, and I'm proud of that. You were like a mother to me. I won't forget it."

"Where you're going you won't remember anything," Stark said.

"I believe in a spirit, Stark. You can be certain mine will be back to make what's left of your life a living hell."

Stark removed his hat. Delaney swallowed hard, closed

her eyes. It was odd how everything came into sharp focus: she could feel every muscle that Buck twitched; the swatting of his tail against flies; the sun on her face; the twittering of the birds in the trees; the flies buzzing around her head; the fluctuation of the rope as Buck shifted his weight to the other hip.

Then she heard her sisters cry out as Stark slapped the buckskin on the rump. She stopped breathing. Buck jerked. But he didn't take one step forward or back. Stark hit him again and swore. Delaney kept her eyes squeezed tight, telling herself it would be over in a second. Any second now. She thought she'd be seeing heaven real soon. Nothing happened.

"Am I gonna choke down?" she asked suddenly. "Or will that rope just snap my neck?"

"Shut up!" Stark hit Buck a good whollop with the flat of his hand. Buck let out with a good, swift kick and got Stark about an inch from his groin. The marshal doubled over, holding himself. If the sky wasn't blue before, it certainly was now. That's the only muscle Buck twitched.

Brett slouched in the saddle, resting her cuffed hands on the saddle horn, deciding to enjoy the turn of events. "Old Buck won't budge unless Delaney tells him to, Eli. And I don't imagine you're going to make her do that."

"Shut up!" He was still bent over from the waist. After a few minutes he straightened up. With one hand he rubbed the back of his neck again; with the other he rubbed his sore spot. "Damn that horse. I'll make him move if I have to put a bullet between his eyes."

"Then you'd just have to drag him out of the way," Delaney ventured.

In a tone that suggested annoyance, Andy said, "Eli, have you got a tick or something on the back of your neck? You certainly have been fussing with it a lot and you're driving me crazy just watching you."

His eyes bulged in sudden alarm. "A tick? How should I know? I can't see back there."

"If you've got a tick," Andy continued, "you could end up with the fever. You'd better have the doctor take a look at it after you get finished here. Maybe you should have left Delaney until last. Old Buck could really slow things down. But I wouldn't advise shooting him. He's a good piece of horseflesh. You might need him and these others to stay ahead of the law."

"Why didn't you tell me about your damned horse?" He lit into Delaney who had finally opened her eyes and was trying to breathe again.

"It never occurred to me," Delaney said honestly. "And Buck's never kicked anybody before in his life. Course, he's never been used for a hanging horse either."

Stark was working at the thing on his neck again and getting increasingly upset.

"Want me to take a look at that?" Brett offered. "You'd feel better if you knew it was only a boil. Delaney isn't going anywhere. Old Buck is so loyal to her he'll stand there until he dies."

Stark didn't like the idea of some blood-sucking creature attached to his head. He tried harder to dig it off.

"You can't get them out that way," Hank said knowledgeably. "You might get its rear end, but the head will stay in and get infected. Of course, if it's one that's carrying the fever, you're probably already infected."

He hated to be beholden to anybody, let alone his prisoners, but he strode over to Hank and the twins. He drew his revolver in one hand, and jerked Hank off her horse with the other. "Look and see what the hell it is—and don't try anything."

217

He put his back to her and lifted up his hat. Hank gingerly parted his graying hair and saw the problem. "It's a tick all right, Eli. A big one. From the looks of it, it's been attached for awhile. I'll bet you've lost a quart of blood, and it's all in his fat little belly."

Stark's face paled. "Get the damned thing off me."

"How am I going to do that, Eli? I'm not going to touch it. You can just leave it in there and have a doctor do it. You've waited this long, it won't hurt to wait a few more hours."

"That's right, Eli," Andy said. "It's probably been on your head for a week or two already."

He was turning green around the gills. "Damn it, Henrietta, use some gloves and pull it out."

"I can't get a grip on it with a pair of gloves. It's not *that* big."

"I've got my tweezers," Brett offered.

Stark's eyes lit with newfound hope. "Then get them, for Christ's sake."

Brett got down from her saddle and brought her saddlebags with her. Andy came along, too. Stark was too upset to tell her to stay put. They joined Hank behind Stark. It took Brett longer than usual to get the buckles undone, but she wasn't in any particular hurry. The longer they delayed, the more likely someone would come to their rescue.

"What's taking so damned long?" Stark looked over his shoulder. "Is your arm broke or something?"

"I'm getting proficient with these cuffs, Eli," Brett replied, "but they don't give a very good range of movement. Be patient. That tick won't suck too much in a couple of minutes."

"Get on with it, damn it."

She rummaged around in her bags some more and finally had to empty the contents on the ground. The mirror that had belonged to their mother slid out along with the tweezers. It was large and solid. And it had been in the family for a long time. Still. . . .

She exchanged a look with Hank and Andy. All three recognized the reflection of good fortune staring back at them.

"I don't think Mama would mind," Andy said.

"What in the hell are you talking about?" Stark snapped.

"Oh, here they are," Brett said cheerfully, gathering up the mirror along with the tweezers. "And to think you wanted me to leave all this stuff behind. Aren't you glad I didn't?"

"Quit talking, damn it, and get that thing off me."

"All right. Here we go, Eli. Just close your eyes and hold real still. This shouldn't hurt very much at all."

Brett brought the mirror down onto his head with tremendous force. Glass shattered. Blood spurted. He plunged forward, shocked and confused. Dazed. He brought his revolver up just as Hank knocked it out of his hand with the saddlebags. He stumbled back. Brett and Andy leaped on him, knocking him all the way down. Brett wrenched the revolver from his hand while Hank pounded his face and head with the saddlebags and Andy kicked him anywhere her feet could make contact. He rolled Hank, easily getting the best of her by sheer weight alone, but he froze when he felt the muzzle of his six-shooter at the back of his head and heard the familiar clicking of the hammer sliding into place.

"Now, I can blow this tick off if you want me to, Eli," Brett threatened. "And I might just have to since those tweezers got lost in the scuffle."

Eli released Hank and rolled to his back.

"You stay right there, marshal," Brett commanded. "Prone is a good position for you about now."

Andy had found a big rock and was holding it over his

head. "Get his keys," she said. "It's his turn to wear these cuffs."

In minutes they were free and holding not only the revolver on Stark but his rifle as well.

"Put your hands behind your head," Brett commanded.

"Oh, that's not nearly good enough," Andy said. "Take off your boots."

Warily, Stark did as he was told.

"Now, the shirt."

His eyes flashed. "Why?"

"Because I said so."

"If you ever want that tick off, you'd better do it," Hank warned.

He did.

"All right." Andy's eyes glowed with satisfaction. "Now the trousers."

"I will not!"

"We could just hang you," Brett suggested.

"Speaking of hanging—" Delaney hollered from the tree.

"Oh, Buck's not going anywhere," Brett hollered back. "Sit tight, little sister. We're almost finished here."

"Yeah, but there's a horsefly the size of a hummingbird biting Buck's shoulder," Delaney lamented, "and I don't know how long he can stand for that."

"Take off your trousers, Eli," Hank reiterated. "If you do, we'll go ahead and remove that tick."

When he was down to his long-handled underwear, Andy took a stroll around him, looking him over like she would a penned mustang. "I guess we could let him keep the long johns on."

Brett tended to agree. "I think you're right, Andy. We wouldn't want to spook Old Buck."

"Damn the bunch of you—"

Hank gathered up the lead rope. "We'll just tie this to your cuffs and take a dally on the saddle horn and let you walk back to town. By the looks of that paunch, a little exercise wouldn't hurt you."

"I can't go into town like this!"

"Oh, all right," Hank conceded. "You can wear your hat."

"What about the tick!"

Brett grinned. "You don't have a tick on your head, Eli. It's just a big old boil."

CHAPTER TWENTY-ONE

RUNNING FREE

The mustangs poured down over the hill like syrup off a stack of buckwheat pancakes. Delaney was right behind them on Buck, running hell-bent for leather. The sun had barely broke the horizon and those broomtails ran away from it, straight for the box canyon and her waiting companions. If there was a heaven, Delaney was sure she had found it.

She pushed the herd hard, never giving them the chance to think of turning back or veering away. From down the long hills came Hank on the left. From the right, Brett and Andy. With perfect timing they flanked the herd, forcing them into the canyon. Brett and Andy pulled up at the canyon entrance to hurry and close the high gate they'd constructed. Delaney and Hank drove the horses on into the rock-walled containment area.

The black stallion skidded to a stop then pranced around his mares. His shrill scream of defiance reverberated off the canyon walls.

Delaney reined to a halt alongside Hank and they sat there in silence enjoying the warmth of spring while watching the wild bunch circle, looking for a way out.

Brett and Andy rode up to join them. Their voices carried in the small canyon, echoing off its stone walls. "Is he the one Bart lost four years ago?"

Hank folded her forearms across the saddle horn. "That's

him. See the brand on his shoulder. Bart will be happy to get him back."

Brett lifted her right leg from the stirrup and crooked her knee around the saddle horn. "Do you think he'll be able to tame him now?"

"I don't know. He ran off with his mother when he was just a colt. He's never had a rope on him."

Andy pushed her hat to the back of her head. "Most times when a horse runs wild it will never give its loyalty to a man. A man can break it, but he never truly tames it. It holds onto the desire to run free."

Delaney thought that philosophy held true for the four of them too. Men might someday win their hearts, put rings on their fingers, might even tame them to a degree, but they'd never take away their desire to run free.

Delaney had seen the changes coming for a long time, but they were closer now, just over the horizon. Hank was still hoping that Bart Breckenridge would get over his shyness and start courting her in earnest. Brett and Andy still had their dreams about San Francisco and Paris, fancy hotels, pretty dresses, rich men.

And Delaney. Well, she couldn't see herself ever leaving the ranch and the little *cabaña*. Besides, with Daddy gone, somebody needed to stay and take care of the place. The only place she planned to go was up to Dutch Flat to visit his grave. She was hoping she could figure a way to get his body back home.

Mainly, after their fiasco with Stark, the four of them had just wanted to come home. They'd missed the mustanging, the freedom of riding the mountains and valleys, of being the daughters of Luke McCall and answering to no one.

As for Stark, he had saved his head that infamous day of the tick only to have his neck stretched a month later for numerous crimes, including horse stealing and the murders of Sheriff Harley and his own deputy.

At least they didn't have to worry about bounty hunters coming after them any more. The U.S. Marshal had posted notices in all the newspapers in California and Nevada that the case against them had been dropped. Stark had sworn to the end that he'd only hired six men: the four who had attacked them at the *cabaña,* and Palmer and Saxton.

Saxton.

There had been plenty of times when Delaney had wondered where Sam Saxton had ridden off to that day after Stark's necktie party. Sam had swung into the saddle and rode up next to her where she stood on the boardwalk all togged out in a fancy dress. He'd leaned down from his saddle, kissed her, then whispered, "There's a good possibility I'll be back this way, Laney."

Her heart had been breaking but she'd never let him know it. "Then maybe I'll see you," she'd said. "*If* I'm still around."

That had been six months ago—six months that seemed more like six years—and she'd seen no sign of him. Nor did she expect to ever again.

She sighed. Sam Saxton was a drifter, a bounty hunter, a man who couldn't settle down with one woman on one plot of ground, no matter what he'd said about buying land and all that nonsense. Maybe she should have told him then that she loved him, but she'd be damned before she'd throw herself at a man. Besides, what did she know about love? Perhaps what she felt for Sam Saxton was merely childish infatuation. Whatever it was, it hurt worse than having a scorpion in your boot.

"I've got a feeling Bart is going to have his hands full with that one," Hank said, speaking of the black stallion.

Delaney gathered her reins. "Don't worry. He'll do fine. Now, ladies, I'd welcome the sight of a dozen eggs and a side of bacon. I feel like a—"

"Digger Indian. Half-starved."

The male voice boomed, echoing into the canyon and drawing their attention to the ridge above. A man sat astride a big horse, silhouetted against the sky with the sun's morning rays behind him. Not far from him, seemingly hanging back, was another rider, broad in the shoulder, sitting his horse in a familiar way.

Delaney's heart tripped. Brett dropped her foot back to the stirrup. Hank gasped.

"My God," Andy whispered. "It looks like . . . Daddy. And Sam Saxton."

Delaney expected the riders to be just another mirage, like those she'd seen before. "It can't be. They said he was dead."

Luke McCall waved and nudged his horse down the narrow trail toward the canyon. Sam Saxton followed.

"It's a miracle," Hank whispered. "Daddy's alive."

Delaney started to cry. Her men had come home.

THE MEMOIRS OF DELANEY MCCALL

December 18, 1920

We tore out of that box canyon faster than chain lightning with a broken link. We nearly smothered Daddy with kisses, and just about drowned him with our tears of joy. He could hardly eat his breakfast for answering all our questions.

*"Palmer said he found a grave with your name on it,"
Hank said. "We all figured you were dead."*

Daddy cradled his cup of coffee in his hands. "I'm sorry I caused you girls distress. I had to do that to get Stark and his bloodhounds off my trail. I wasn't able to do it myself, so Laura helped me."

"Laura?" Our four voices were so much in harmony, we sounded like a church choir.

A flush rose in Daddy's cheeks. "The doc. You remember her?"

"We remember she was real pretty," I insinuated.

Daddy got a faraway look. "Yes, she was that. I hope you all don't mind that I invited her down for a visit."

I had once thought I would never want Daddy to marry again, but seeing that look of longing on his face made me realize that he needed a woman the same as the rest of us needed a man. I sensed that if Laura Hogan came to Monterey, she wouldn't be leaving.

Once again, those winds of change brushed over me. I understood them better now, though, and I didn't object to see-

ing them advance on the horizon.

Daddy went on to tell us that when he'd gotten strong enough he'd headed to Virginia City only to find us gone. "I ran into Sam," he said, glancing over at the ex-bounty hunter. "He was running your old place and hauling in money hand over fist. Said he had a fortune to make because he intended on coming back to California to buy a ranch, settle down and raise a family. Said he had a girl in mind, if she'd wait for him."

Daddy gave me a knowing smile. I went to work on my eggs and bacon and pretended I didn't have any romantic interest in Sam at all, and no idea what Daddy was talking about. Between the bacon and eggs, though, I sneaked a peek at Sam and saw that he was looking at me with a silly grin on his face.

Daddy and Sam got to be good friends in Virginia City so Sam told him about our escapades with Palmer and Stark. Sam confided in me later that it had upset him a lot that he hadn't been able to rescue me from my near hanging. As for his fortune, he didn't quite make it in Virginia City, but he made a good start so he didn't go back. I think he was afraid if he left again, I might meet another fellow and forget about him. I didn't tell him that he wouldn't have had to worry about that. Best to keep a man uncertain so he won't take you for granted.

Nobody ever saw hide nor hair of Blade Palmer again. We often wondered if his ghost was still wandering around on Walker Pass, or if he just took off, deciding he'd rather go afoot than contend with the daughters of Luke McCall. We were a hard bunch to keep a dally on.

Daddy was sorely disappointed that Stark turned bad and met his fate at the end of a rope, even if it was fitting for all he'd put us through, and the people of Hawk's Point. A lot of his sadness over the incident was for the loss of innocence we all

227

suffered, and maybe a little for days gone by. Days that we knew were never going to come back when those winds of change struck us with their full force.

We spent the meantime in our saddles, ropes coiled and ready, waiting for those mustangs to break over the rim running. We enjoyed those days more than any before or since because we had acquired a great appreciation for being alive and together.

Well, it is time to end my story. I leave the memories of the past to you, my children and grandchildren. Tend them well, as you do your own. I know that someday you will understand their true worth. Now I bid you farewell.

Your grandmother,
Delaney McCall Saxton

Delaney set her pen aside and watched the ink dry on her signature. She wiped a tear from her eye. Damn, but she missed the bunch of them, and missed those days of running free. She'd give her eye teeth if she could go back. She'd give *all* her teeth, or what was left of them, if she had everyone here to sit on the front porch at sundown, drink strong coffee, and reminisce. That was the flaw in being the youngest; you were left alone in the end.

She figured she'd be seeing Sam and Daddy and the girls real soon, though. As a matter of fact, she wouldn't be surprised if Sam was saddling up Old Buck right now and laying out her riding togs, getting ready for her to come home.

She released a contented sigh and closed the notebook.

She'd be with him soon now. Very soon.